LILAC—
lovely and well-loved...

She had promised to be home by Sunday
night if her friend Victoria would help. A
difficult deception—to pretend Lilac was ill
in the house when all that terrifying week-
end Lilac was really gone—gone away to
an unknown somewhere.

Only Victoria and the stolid, loyal nurse
knew Lilac had disappeared.

Then the nurse was slaughtered, viciously,
with a sickle. And in the shadow of a fright-
filled night, Victoria came face to face with
the murderer!

THE
SECOND
SICKLE

Ursula Curtiss

A KANGAROO BOOK
PUBLISHED BY POCKET BOOKS NEW YORK

THE SECOND SICKLE

Dodd, Mead edition published 1950

POCKET BOOK edition published April, 1977

The characters, places, incidents and situations in this book are imaginary and have no relation to any person, place or actual happening

This POCKET BOOK edition includes every word contained in the original, higher-priced edition. It is printed from brand-new plates made from completely reset, clear, easy-to-read type.
POCKET BOOK editions are published by
POCKET BOOKS,
a division of Simon & Schuster, Inc.,
A GULF+WESTERN COMPANY
630 Fifth Avenue,
New York, N.Y. 10020.
Trademarks registered in the United States and other countries.

ISBN: 0-671-80951-2.
This POCKET BOOK edition is published by arrangement with Dodd, Mead & Company. Copyright, 1950, by Ursula R. Curtiss.

Cover illustration by Howard Koslow.

Printed in the U.S.A.

THE
SECOND
SICKLE

Prologue

The hands moved quietly in the twilit gloom of the shed. They were gloved in black leather, darker than the shadows around them, and their search was serene and patient and infinitely careful.

A scythe leaned in a cobwebbed corner. The supple black fingers of one hand closed around the handle and shifted it noiselessly to the wall. Beyond it a dusty wooden box was stuffed carelessly with long-unused tools of carpentry and gardening: a claw-headed hammer, a pair of heavy hedge clippers, a rusty iron bolt from some forgotten door. A vise, a giant pliers . . . one questing hand was sharply still as a shaft of light bloomed suddenly into the shed.

The little high window at the end of the living room . . . of course. The shed was attached to the back of the house, and the curtains of the window were not quite drawn. Quietly, quietly—the gloved hands, looking oddly lifeless, hung against the inner wall of the shed.

A glowing slice of living room stretched away between the curtains. A Persian rug seethed soft flame and gold and blue. The edge of a long gilt-framed mirror, the slim polished legs of an end table, an arm of deep blue couch—and then a hand, with a single shining cuff of gold bracelet above it, reaching out to flip up the silver lid of a cigarette box.

The girl in the living room—she came into view a moment later—seemed restless. She was obviously alone in the room. She took a cigarette and bent forward a little to pick up the lighter and radiance from the lamp caught the swing of shining fair hair, the plume of smoke, the wink of the bracelet as she replaced the lighter. After a second the cigarette went down in a heavy glass ashtray. The girl moved away. An aimless note sounded from the invisible piano, followed by a light angry crash of the keys.

But she hadn't gone yet. She was at the window, looking out into the deepening dusk, the neglected cigarette making broken ringlets of blue-white smoke under the lamp. Distantly, a telephone rang; she moved out of sight, came swiftly back to retrieve the cigarette and left the room.

And now the slanting beam of light in the shed was a help instead of a menace. The hands were quicker and more careless; a screwdriver tumbled out of the box in the corner, another hammer, a tin of nails . . .

There was the sickle, over against the other wall, leaning in a negligent curve of silver. Not rusted. (There must be no rust.) In a single stooping, scooping motion, black leather fingers closed gently over the handle.

Seconds later, there were only shadows in the shed.

CHAPTER 1

VICTORIA DEVLIN picked up the library phone. In the fractional second of action that made a living thing out of the coiled wire she thought; It's Lilac. It's Sunday night and it must be Lilac, and I can leave this dreadful house and go home. . . . "Hello?"

A voice said, "Nurse Corey . . . ? Oh, Miss Devlin."

It wasn't Lilac. Maddeningly, it was Simon Halliday, the man to whom Lilac was engaged. Victoria felt the expectation go out of her and listened to her own polite well-rehearsed phrases; "Lilac's sleeping right now. . . . No, just about the same, I think. Nurse Corey is with her. . . . If you like, but I'm quite sure you won't be able to see her tonight. No, I don't think there's anything you can bring her. . . ." She hung up.

Standing there with the phone quiet and harmless again under her hand, aware of the faint spicy smell of wood smoke and the fragrance of roses, Victoria thought suddenly and clearly, I don't like this, and I never did. Where is she?

The silence of Lilac Thall's house struck mockingly back at her. Not for the first time, Victoria wondered why Lilac had stayed on here after her sister had married nearly two years ago. Probably because she had been unable to dispose of it; huge brick piles requiring lavish maintenance and a staff of servants were a drug on the present real-estate market. The once-wealthy Thalls, Victoria knew, had had only the house and a tiny income to leave to their daughters—and Lilac would of course feel none of her own reluctance in occupying these shadowy spaces alone. She had, after all, grown up in these high-ceilinged rooms and narrow halls, had played in the little damp garden and on the shaggy hump of hill above the harbor. Besides, she often had someone staying with her; her infrequent letters spoke airily of people whom Victoria assumed she should remember and never did. In any case, during the last few months Lilac had undoubtedly spent a good deal of time with her fiancé's family.

But where was she now? It was Sunday night and nearly six o'clock, with wind-sharp November darkness closing in. And Lilac had said, her face taut and strained with pleading, "I'll be back by Sunday night at the latest, Victoria. I swear it. It's only for the week-end—"

Only for the week-end, thought Victoria wryly, but as soon as the announcement that Lilac was ill had been made, the two and a half days had seemed to multiply themselves into twenty. The phone ringing, the questions, the alarm and concern, the dangerous periods when people were actually in the house, wanting to go up to the sickroom and having to be stopped, lingering over their solicitousness, sending flowers and calves'-foot jelly and fond messages.

For a girl who was hundreds of miles away and who trusted, apparently, not a single one of them.

"It won't work," Victoria had said.

"It will," Lilac had answered flatly—and, so far, it had. Perhaps because the sight of a sterile white uniform was traditionally daunting, perhaps because it seemed incredible that gaunt, severe Nurse Corey would carry up trays of frothy eggnog and homemade beef broth and slender golden points of toast only to consume them herself in the emptiness of the third floor sickroom.

Victoria, from the beginning, hadn't wanted anything to do with the plan, particularly in the face of Lilac's mutinous refusal to explain her motives. But she had been at school with Lilac, had been a guest during several summers at the Thall home in Seacastle, the house that seemed so big and strange now; had kept in touch with Lilac over the years and miles and changing interests that separated them.

And only a Central Park statue could have refused Lilac on the night when she had come to Victoria's New York apartment, with hysteria under a face of calm and desperation behind her pleading. "I've got to get away from Seacastle for a few days without anyone knowing. I've got to . . ."

The library clock struck six in a hollow, tremulous tenor.

Lilac must surely be on her way back to Seacastle now, having accomplished—what? Victoria stared down at the desk as though the answer lay there in shining wood and leather-cornered blotter, orderly ranks of pencils and a blind, blank calendar. She had thought at first, vaguely, that Lilac's mission concerned a man in some way—a connection to be severed, farewells to be said now that she wore Simon Halliday's diamond on her hand. She had realized almost instantly that that wasn't it, that Lilac's goodbyes, if she had any to say, would be crisp and kind and final. She had at times an unthinking black-and-whiteness, an innocently ruthless quality that manifested itself in phrases like, "Have you been ill? Oh, I guess it's that hat. . . ." or "Your slipcovers look marvelous. Tell me, did you ever think of stripes? They do wonders for these dark cellary rooms. . . ."

No, it wasn't a lingering lover's farewell. And it didn't really matter in any case, because—Victoria looked at the clock—it was five minutes after six, and her disturbing sojourn was drawing to a close. Meanwhile, Simon Halliday had said he would be over at around eight, and Nurse Corey would have to be armed with a fresh batch of explanations.

In the living room, half aware that she was deliberately postponing the dark journey upstairs, Victoria spent another idle moment in pulling back flowered linen to glance out at the night, retrieving a puffy purple aster that had fallen from a bowl on the rosewood desk, crushing her cigarette in a heavy glass ashtray. Above the first floor, the Thall house was draughty and echoing, with the black mouths of unused bedrooms gaping emptily off the dim landings, and the stairs leading grayly up to the huge third floor sickroom where Nurse Corey kept vigil with her non-existent patient. No; at night it wasn't a pleasant trip.

Nerves, thought Victoria. Just because you haven't a crosstown bus snoring under the window and taxi horns making a comfortable pattern in the distance and apartment house lights suspended in the sky. Just because there's only a great dim house with two women alone in it, and the lonely sound of the sea and that blasted grandfather clock. . . .

The little high window that looked out into the shed showed a narrow wedge of black between flowered curtains. Victoria crossed the room and pulled the curtains to. Then she went out into the hall and briskly up the dark staircase.

Second floor: a battered mahogany table with a lamp and a telephone extension, two portraits of joyless, long-dead Thalls, three unused bedrooms and the one she slept in. More stairs, winding dimly to the top of the house. No night light up here on the tiny hall table; Nurse Corey and her Boston thrift, thought Victoria grimly, and felt her way cautiously around the turn of the stairs and up to the top.

There was darkness all around her, thick and anonymous. The main part of the house, the lighted safety lay below, two floors away. A thin crack of light gleamed under the sickroom door; Victoria fumbled her way toward it, ashamed of a wave of gladness and relief. She called crisply, "Nurse? . . . Nurse Corey?" because a human sound seemed suddenly imperative in the waiting stillness of the house, and opened the bedroom door.

The room was empty.

It took her a moment to realize it; the room was vast, covering more than half the top of the house. A four-poster bed spread with white candlewick, a pillow-piled chaise longue, Turkey red armchairs, a bureau, a plump green ottoman didn't begin to fill its dim serene length. Six small recessed windows, petticoated in starched blue and white, looked out on darkness, looked in on lighted emptiness. Nurse Corey's knitting, an improbable mass of navy blue, was huddled in an armchair.

But where was the nurse? Victoria was all at once more aware than ever of the isolation of the third floor. Standing in the lighted silence, staring at the untenanted bed, she felt a spurt of irritation at Nurse Corey, who must have gone out without telling her. It was an incredibly stupid thing to do. If someone had come—Simon, or Simon's aunt or brother, or Lilac's anxious, vigilant sister . . .

Behind her the bedroom door swung open. For a moment, Nurse Corey and Victoria stared at each other: the older woman white-capped, her dark eyes blazing in a gaunt, lined, remote face, her fingers still tight on the glass doorknob; Victoria slender and questioning in the middle of the room.

Nurse Corey spoke first. She closed the door carefully behind her and said in her low, slightly harsh voice, "I'm sorry if I startled you. I was looking for some addresses in an old book in the bedroom I used to have. Did you want something?"

"Simon Halliday is coming here at eight o'clock," Victoria said. "He's very determined to see Lilac, or get another medical opinion. I thought I'd better let you know, so that if he insists on talking to you ..."

"Thank you," said Nurse Corey, nodding. "Eight o'clock. I don't suppose Lilac will be back by then? Or maybe—?"

"She might be on her way." Victoria watched the nurse pick up her dark blue knitting and start to work neatly and efficiently, as though she had never put it down. Odd, she thought. She could have sworn that the second floor rooms were all in darkness when she came upstairs—but two of the bedroom doors had been closed, and with the night light glowing on the landing she mightn't have noticed the lamplit line of a doorway. Besides, why should the woman lie?

"Won't you sit down?" said Nurse Corey politely. "Though I suppose we'd better have some dinner and get it over with if Mr. Halliday is coming."

In the big old-fashioned kitchen they set the white-painted metal table against the windows; it seemed pointless to light and arrange the dark dining room. Victoria sliced the cold roast beef the maid had cooked the day before and Nurse Corey peeled potatoes and put water on for tea, her face withdrawn and preoccupied. That again was odd, Victoria thought, lifting plates out of the cupboard; here in the kitchen of Lilac's house in Seacastle were the only two people whom she had trusted with her secret, and yet the common bond of conspiracy and fondness for Lilac that ought to have existed between them did not. They might have been strangers who mildly disliked each other's looks, uncongenial passengers compelled to share the same seat on a bus, for all the sympathy there was between them.

It didn't matter; Nurse Corey was, Victoria knew, unshakable in her loyalty to Lilac. She had been holding heads and administering pills in the Thall family for over fifteen years. When Lilac had fallen off the shed roof, when Mrs. Thall had had rheumatic fever, when Millicent had broken her arm, Nurse Corey had always been there, cold and aloof and unflusterable, as though sudden illness were an indecent prank which she did not intend to dignify by recognition. Of them all Lilac was the only one she cared about.

They washed the dishes in silence; it had been decided that Angie Harris, the maid who came in by the day, might grow curious if she spent too much time in the house. Victoria put the cups away with one eye on the clock. If Lilac's cab should arrive while Simon Halliday were here . . . but there were other entrances: the kitchen, the glass doors in the dining room, the garage. And certainly when Lilac did turn up she'd have guile enough to be on the watch for visitors. . . .

Nurse Corey shook out a dishtowel and hung it neatly to dry. "I'd better not be down here when Mr. Halliday comes. You'll let me know?" Her firm rubbery tread took her out of the kitchen, across the hall, up the stairs and out of hearing.

It was a quarter of eight. Victoria snapped off the kitchen light and went upstairs to her own room. Halfway to the bureau against the far wall, she paused.

She had—hadn't she?—left the closet door closed; carelessly open doors were one of her few tidy aberrations. The door was slightly ajar now, no more than three inches, but still . . . Nurse Corey had been on the second floor two hours ago. Looking for some old addresses in the room she had once occupied, she had said—but she had never had this room. It had always, as far as Victoria knew, been Lilac's.

Inside the closet, on the top shelf, her striped hat box was at a precarious tilt and a taffeta scarf had fallen to the floor. Angie Harris, thought of Victoria with a little rush of relief, Angie Harris with her bright mouse's eyes; the maid had been curious and had looked over her wardrobe, that was all.

The sound of the sea was clearer here. Victoria opened the windows that gave on the hill and the washing waves beyond it, and spent a swift minute and a half with lipstick and powder and comb. Another medical opinion,

Simon had said pleasantly. . . . But Lilac would be here tonight, or by morning at the latest. And a little more than a month from now, her urgent and secret mission accomplished, she would be married to Simon Halliday in satin and serenity and her great-grandmother's wedding veil. Victoria gave the mirror a sardonic look and went down to the doorbell and the bridegroom-to-be.

Simon Halliday, founder and president of Halliday, Pierce and Brittain, Advertising, took up more of the hall than one man should. He threw his topcoat and hat on the table, tossed a florist's box and two books to the chair beside it and turned to Victoria; abruptly the chill emptiness around them was full of stir and energy. "How's Lilac?" he asked. "Can I see her now, or is she still asleep?"

Victoria looked away from the long faintly cynical face and the cool measuring eyes. "She's asleep, as far as I know, at least she was when I was upstairs a few minutes ago. But I can call Nurse Corey, and—"

"No hurry," said Simon Halliday, and followed her into the living room.

He's here in the house, thought Victoria, looking a little wildly about her, and he doesn't want to see Nurse Corey right away and what am I do to with him? She said strainedly, "Would you like some coffee?"

"Not if it's a nuisance."

"Not at all," said Victoria brightly, and started for the kitchen.

It was then that the phone rang, a single echoing peal, made more startling by the abruptness with which it was cut off. Victoria had stopped and half-turned with dangerous, instinctive eagerness; aware again of Simon behind her, she went on into the kitchen, her mind in a sudden whirl.

Was it Lilac—or a casual wrong number? A glance at the kitchen clock took the edge of expectancy away. Lilac's sister had said she might phone this evening. . . . In silence Victoria put water and coffee in the percolator, plugged it into the wall socket and took cups and saucers from the cupboard with an efficient clatter, aware all the time of the speculative eyes upon her.

"Going to rain," remarked Simon pleasantly.

"Oh . . . ?"

"We often get rain at this time of year. That is," said

Simon explanatorily, "if we don't get a heavy fog. Or both."

After she's married, Victoria thought abstractedly, Lilac will at least have plenty of interesting conversation about the weather. She filled the sugar bowl and said, "I suppose . . . you're right on the coast here. . . ."

"But I keep forgetting," went on Simon's smooth voice, "that you know Seacastle quite well. . . . How sick is Lilac, really?"

Victoria put the sugar bowl down without a tremor, in spite of jarring inward shock. She turned to Simon, cocking her head and her brows with a considering air. "I'm afraid you'd have to ask Nurse Corey that. I do know that she isn't eating, and that she's under a mild sedative a lot of the time. . . ."

"Feverish, too, I suppose," said Simon abruptly.

"Well, yes, that's one of the—"

"And fairly weak, I presume, as she isn't allowed visitors."

"Naturally."

"Then," said Simon, without a flicker of expression, "what was she doing driving around Seacastle at dusk on a raw damp day like this?"

CHAPTER 2

"DRIVING. . . . Oh, no, she couldn't have been," said Victoria after a stunned moment of silence. For the first time in nearly three days she could let her face and voice relax and show the astonishment that was really there. "Lilac wouldn't—couldn't . . ."

Careful here. Impossible to say, 'Lilac wouldn't dream of showing herself to any of you before tomorrow with the proper sickroom setting. Not when she went to such elaborate lengths to deceive you, not when she was terrified at the idea of your finding out, any of you, that she hasn't been upstairs in this house for more than three days.'

The coffee leaped in a brown froth in the percolator top and seethed and leaped again. Victoria took the plug out of the socket and went on, keeping her voice cool and practical, "In the first place, Lilac's in no condition to be up and around, let alone out driving. And even if she could manage it, which I doubt, Nurse Corey and I have been here all afternoon. It must have been someone who looked like Lilac, someone—"

"Yes," said Simon casually and nodded, and watched her pour coffee into the two cups. "It must have been someone else. In Lilac's car. In the scarf we bought together a few days ago."

"Cream?" asked Victoria stonily, and when Simon

11

said no, took the cups and started for the living room, her carriage erect and unhurried, her mind bewildered and angry. If, after the scene in her own New York apartment last Thursday night, when Lilac had asked her to do this preposterous thing; if after the three days of lies and subterfuge and feigned concern she had gone through, Lilac had come boldly back to Seacastle in daylight . . . But she wouldn't.

Anger melted and worry took its place. There was something wrong here, something more wrong than Simon could know, something that had to be approached on tiptoe. Lilac had said on Thursday night, gold lamplight striping one pale slanted cheek, "If anyone found out, I think I'd—" She'd stopped there, with a sharp desperate movement of her hands that was more frightening than any conclusion in words.

Victoria sipped her coffee and reached for a cigarette and smiled at Simon Halliday, as if something logical and reassuring had just occurred to her. "Lilac probably lent her keys to someone, knowing she wouldn't be using the car herself," she said. "Millicent, or your cousin Olive, or any one of her friends. . . ."

Simon's voice was dry. "Lilac has a very low regard for Millicent's driving ability. And Olive has the station wagon, and besides, I know the way Lilac drives. But—" his voice died away and his head went back a little stiffly, as though a sudden recollection had jerked at his memory. Then that was gone too, and the smile he gave Victoria was disarming and a little apologetic. "I didn't mean this to turn into a third-degree. It's just that I've been concerned about Lilac and then, this afternoon when—I suppose it was the scarf that jolted me, as much as the car."

"The scarf?" Out of one morass and into another. If she could only get away from Simon Halliday's observing eyes. It didn't matter, any of it, because Lilac would be in bed in the sickroom by morning and could very well, Victoria thought grimly, do her own explaining. But meanwhile it was just as easy to be undone at the eleventh hour as in the first bold beginning of the deception. Be careful for just an hour or two more. . . . "Well, scarves," said Victoria, moving her cigarette in a small deprecating arc. "They can look pretty much alike, don't you think? Particularly at dusk?"

"We bought this one together, at that little place on

Sea Street," said Simon. His face was puzzled. "The woman had stocked only a few of them and Lilac got the last. It was one of those squares, silk and wool I think, imported from somewhere, with a handful of gold sequins in one corner. Pink. On Lilac it was—"

Yes, thought Victoria, it would have been. Lilac with her straight glossy black hair, her bold, gay pirate's face, her polished light gray eyes—and a shy cool pink coif to bring it all into sharper focus.

She said, laughing, "I wouldn't tell Lilac, if I were you; she probably thinks she has the only pink one in Seacastle." That was clever, that had the ring of illogical truth. I'll get back to New York, thought Victoria, and I won't be able to tell anyone my name without hedging and sparring and a few cunning aliases. Back to New York ... soon, now. Tomorrow.

"Good evening, Mr. Halliday," Nurse Corey said from the doorway. Simon was on his feet, greeting the nurse and inquiring about Lilac, and Victoria escaped to the kitchen with the coffee cups. Behind her as she retreated Nurse Corey's voice said, "Tomorrow, perhaps. Her temperature's down, and we're hoping . . . ."

Who had been driving Lilac's car, wearing Lilac's pink scarf? Lilac hadn't meant to lend anyone her car. She had said she would leave the keys in her calf handbag, that it would look odd if for any reason someone wanted them and they were missing. And the calf handbag, Victoria knew, was somewhere on the first floor of the house; she remembered seeing it, casually and unnoticingly, half a dozen times over the week-end. In the library? On the second shelf of the magazine table in the living room ... on the dining room buffet?

There were almost as many intervals when the car could have been returned to the garage, late on that dim windy afternoon, without their being aware of it. The garage was perhaps thirty feet away, behind the house at the kitchen side, an ivy-smothered red brick structure. The driveway tilted down from the road, so that you could coast in with no motor humming, no headlamps beaconing.

Victoria put the cups and saucers away and turned sharply as Simon said, in the doorway, "I've just been telling Nurse Corey you ought to get out for a little air."

Out for a little air—she had done enough dodging and lying and smiling with Simon Halliday. "It's very thoughtful of you," Victoria began stiffly, "but I've some letters to do and—"

Behind Simon, at his shoulder, Nurse Corey broke flatly in. "It would really do you good, I think, Miss Devlin. You've been in the house so much the past two days . . . and perhaps if it wouldn't be too much trouble you could pick up that sandalwood soap Lilac likes."

Was there a message in the remote dark eyes under the graying hair and the nurses' cap? Victoria watched her fleetingly and then came forward, smiling over a quick inner surge of excitement. The phone call a little while ago hadn't been a wrong number or a solicitous inquiry about Lilac. It had been Lilac herself; she was on her way here and the house had to be cleared. It was all but over now. Victoria's voice was gay as she said, "It would be nice. I'll get my coat."

Lilac coming back, this mysterious and troubling interval in her life dealt with and forgotten; Victoria caught herself on the edge of humming and went out into the thick chilly November dark with Simon's hand at her elbow. Down the little flagged walk to the driveway, blurry underfoot with wet fallen leaves, into Simon's car, with the window down so that fresh cold air rushed at her face, delightful as water on a thirsty throat.

"Just anywhere?" said Simon looking at her across darkness. "Soap for Lilac, and then a drink?"

The narrow tilting streets of the town were nearly deserted, the roads shimmering faintly with the dampness of mist off the harbor. Victoria bought sandalwood soap from a sleepy clerk in Seacastle's only drug store and got back into the car, still feeling free and gay and unburdened. When Simon asked tentatively, "Cold enough for a hot buttered rum?" she said, "Oh, easily," and leaned back comfortably against the cushions.

And then her comfort was rudely stripped away. Simon told her, non-committally and almost idly, that earlier in the week the police had found Lilac asleep behind the wheel of her car drawn up at the side of the road. She was apparently under the influence of a drug.

Drugs . . . Lilac . . . Victoria was horrified.

"It was on Wednesday," Simon said. "Our offices in Boston are being expanded so I was home that day. We all went to lunch at the Harbor Inn—"

"All?" echoed Victoria blankly. The sense of oppression was back in her, because it was on Thursday, one day later, that Lilac had come to her so desperately in New York. . . .

"My Aunt Grace," Simon was saying, "and Rufe—you remember my brother Rufe, don't you? And Millicent, of course," was there a slight ironic stress at the mention of Lilac's placid, devoted, protective sister? "and Freddy Spencer—Millicent married him, you know. Olive was there, too, and some wild-eyed kid, Storrow I think his name is, who's had a frustrated passion for Lilac ever since his Eton collar days. Lilac's sorry for him and I suppose she thought it would be easier to have a farewell lunch with him in the middle of a crowd. And then—"

After lunch, Simon said, turning a steep corner with care, the rest of them had drifted off and he and Lilac had sat over a liqueur for a while, discussing wedding arrangements until Lilac had to go to her hairdresser's. She had driven off in her own car and had remained at the salon for perhaps an hour and a half. After that she had gone for a short drive before starting home.

"It was around five-fifteen," Simon said, "when some woman on Honeyman's Lane, just outside town, called the police to say there was a car with a drunken driver in it parked in her hedge. It was Lilac—and she wasn't drunk, she was under the influence of some opiate or other. When she came to she said she'd taken several aspirin to get rid of a headache when she was at the hairdresser's. She couldn't remember stopping the car, couldn't remember anything."

After an incredulous moment Victoria said, "But she might have been—hurt."

Simon parked the car outside the Cabot House. "It's a miracle she wasn't. Why she didn't hit a tree, or another car . . . Careful, I think I've parked you in a puddle."

The Cabot House, flickeringly candlelit, was on Water Street, near one tip of the half-moon that the harbor carved in the rocky shore. Victoria sat in a tall-backed booth near the door while Simon went to the bar to order drinks. She hardly heard the rustle and splash of the waves beneath the window, she was remembering that Lilac had always had a profound fear and distrust of sedatives of any kind. And to take several aspirin when she knew she had to drive . . .

None of my business, thought Victoria, trying uneasily

to shake herself free; curious and rather frightening, but still none of my business. I've done what Lilac asked me to do, and it's nearly over. A steaming glass was set down before her. Simon, dropping into the seat opposite, said abruptly, "By the way, Millicent doesn't know about the police finding Lilac asleep in her car—or at least she doesn't know the whole thing, and I'd just as soon she didn't. She'd only fret and hover, and Millicent," his mouth made a grimace, "is a little heavy on the wing. But I thought you ought to know. That's why I was so worried when I thought I saw Lilac in her car this afternoon, particularly with that fellow from the sanitarium still at large. Although by this time—"

Sanitarium . . . it went through Victoria with a bewildering chill. She said, staring, "What sanitarium? Do you mean that a patient escaped?"

Simon stared back, incredulous in turn. "Good Lord—didn't you know? But you've been in the house all the time, of course. I'll say a patient escaped. . . ." He told her, then, and gradually the fear and horror that had paralyzed the town for the past five days came almost tangibly into the booth.

Bellemarsh Sanitarium, Simon explained, was a huddle of antique wooden buildings on an otherwise deserted spur of Seacastle Point. The authorities there had frequently petitioned for more modern equipment, but nothing had been done because the sanitarium housed mainly alcoholics, nervous-breakdown cases and other harmless patients. One small isolated wing with heavily barred windows was set aside for the dangerously insane, and William Fowler, a paranoiac, was the only inmate of the violent wing when he escaped.

"As a matter of fact he was due for transfer to the big state asylum," Simon said, "and they think now that he found out about it somehow. Anyway, he'd been ill, or pretending to be ill, for a couple of weeks—apparently they had to coax him even to eat. There was a new attendant on duty the night of the thirteenth, I think it was, and I suppose he'd been told about Fowler's condition and wasn't prepared to be half-strangled as soon as he stuck his head into the cell. He didn't come to enough to raise any outcry for the better part of an hour, and by that time Fowler was well away."

"But . . . the sanitarium officials, the police—"

Simon shrugged. "They put a police block on the causeway leading out to the Point, of course, but apparently Fowler had gotten a lift with some unsuspecting motorist. And they tried to tone it down, in the beginning; they didn't want a general panic on their hands as well. That was before they found the Brainard child—and, later on the same day, Wednesday, an elderly woman, a librarian. Coroner's office said they'd both been killed with a sickle."

A sickle. . . . "I wish you wouldn't," said Victoria, feeling ill. "Anyway, he must be miles away by now. Whoever did that wouldn't dare stay in a little town like Seacastle where everyone's hunting for him. . . ." The great dark Thall house, remembered her mind. The wet rustling garden behind it, the hill that sloped down to the bay. And Nurse Corey there alone.

"I'm sorry," Simon said instantly, with a glance at her whitened face. "I wouldn't have brought it up except that I thought you knew. Ready?"

It was windy outside, and dark. Simon said, "Wait here, I'll get the car," and she stood in the shadow of a cedar beside the entrance, stiffening herself against the cold and the horror of what Simon had just told her.

". . . fool, you stupid fool," said a woman's voice on the other side of the cedar. "I told you you wouldn't be able to get in to see her. What do you think that nurse is for? And what good would it do anyway? She'd only tell your dear friend Simon."

"Listen, Millie—" A man's voice, soft and ugly. "You're in this just as deep as I am, that's a little thing you seem to keep forgetting."

"Please . . . don't . . . call . . . me . . . Millie." The words were slow and savage, temper held by a hair, and Victoria, standing very still and shocked in the concealing dimness beside the cedar, went rocketing back in memory . . . five years, six? It was Millicent Thall who spoke, now Millicent Spencer, solidly pink and pretty and placid, who didn't like to be teased. Even at twenty-three she would stamp her foot in petulance and say, "Please. I wish you wouldn't call me Millie. . . ."

What would Lilac "only tell" Simon?

Simon's car pulled up, the headlights carving a long gold track across the entrance, and at the same moment Millicent and Freddy Spencer came into view off on the left. Without conscious thought Victoria tucked her face into shadow and fumbled with her handbag until the Cabot House door had swung to behind them. Then she walked out to the waiting car.

If Simon had seen Millicent and her husband he didn't mention it. The drive back to the Thall house was silent and sombre; Simon had retreated into impersonal formality and Victoria was preoccupied with her own disturbing thoughts, about Lilac and when Lilac would appear and set her free. Seacastle with the vague spectre of a killing lunatic at large was becoming more and more unpalatable by the minute. A cruising police car and a patrolman roaming along Water Street were hardly reassuring in the light of what she now knew.

The third floor lights still gleamed dimly as the car pulled into the driveway. Around the front door the humped shadows of rhododendron bushes made secret stirring motions under the wind; Victoria was gratefully conscious of Simon beside her on the dark slippery path across the lawn. She thanked him and said goodnight, standing in the hall, and Simon nodded without speaking and handed her the package of sandalwood soap. He said casually, "Lock up after me, will you?" and was gone. Almost at once the headlights of his car swept an arc across the lawn and the night came blotting back.

Victoria took off her coat and gloves and locked the door carefully before she dimmed the light in the hall. The glass doors in the dining room, the kitchen door, the bolt on the cellar door that was stiff and needed prodding; she made herself attend to them all with conscientious fingers. Then she thought, Lilac—and let the excitement inside her spill over and began to run up the stairs.

The sickle cut keenly but not quickly; there was time for the ripping start of a scream out of the pain-filled throat. But the fingers inside black leather were nimble and strong. The sickle rose again, scooping through the half-dark, and drew a shorter, surer arc. Under the dim moonless sky the blade caught no reflection at all.

CHAPTER 3

SEACASTLE, which could flare into profane indignation over the closing of a grass-grown right of way, had been cloaked and secretive and peculiarly silent now for nearly a week.

Normally it was a brusque, busy, sour little town which had long since reverted from the chic and sheltered summer resort of the twenties. There weren't even any Wealthy People any more. The yachts had moved up the coast to Gracie Harbor and the great ugly homes on the Point were shuttered, most of them, and discreetly for sale. Seacastle was itself again, with its steep mystifyingly one-way streets, its old shingled houses blanched to the color of moonlight, its unsuspected back gardens that a short time ago had shown flashing slices of grass and flowers and trees. Along High Street, the few display windows leaned heavily to sou'westers and hip boots. Along Water Street, at pungent intervals, came the piercing scent of ripe lobster bait.

Sergeant Harry Tansill loved it.

But, late on that fog-filled Monday morning when Patrolman Charley Peters came clattering into the tiny police station on High Street, the sergeant's heart sank. He knew, almost before Peters told him. And he was almost certain what they would find: the stiffened body, the viciously mutilated throat, the bloodied clothing. The sickle—if the coroner was right in his stubborn and grisly hunch—gone, with the blade wiped fastidiously clean and readied again.

Without another look at Patrolman Peters' gasping white face, Sergeant Tansill called Bellemarsh Sanitarium and informed them of what had happened, talked briefly, pushed the phone away and put on his coat. "Seems to me there was somebody else, a friend, staying at the Thall house with her," he said. "Better go up there and make it official."

Three quarters of an hour later, Victoria Devlin looked down through the chilly silver fog and said in a dry whisper, "Oh, yes. That's Nurse Corey," and moved blindly away to stand shivering in the cold and staring fiercely at nothing until Sergeant Tansill led her gently back up the hill and into the house.

Inside the girl turned to him. She said in an unnaturally quiet voice, "Excuse me, Sergeant. I think I'm going to be—" and fled up the stairs. Sergeant Tansill, his pleasant, usually affable face morose, looked after her a minute and then went into the living room.

First the Brainard girl, a plump, flaxen-haired child of twelve, on her way home from school in broad daylight, taking a shortcut through Cowper's Grove. Then the librarian, the elderly Miss Elizabeth Cossett—that was after dark, like this latest one must have been. No one in town had reported a missing sickle, although householders in the areas of both crimes had been urged to check, and inquiries were still being made. Furthermore, a cold snap had set in last night, and Sergeant Tansill thought moodily that it would complicate things for the coroner, and then shook his head to clear it.

What was the point of all this slaughter—where, rather, was the danger signal, the single factor that turned the deranged mind to killing violence? Was it merely all lone, vulnerable women? Was it more simply anyone who crossed his path and therefore represented the threat of capture? It wasn't as if they were all attractive young girls, Sergeant Tansill reasoned, staring emptily about the glowing room; it wasn't as if—

The girl was back. She looked even paler now but more composed, the fair hair smooth against her white cheeks, her mouth level and noncommittal, her fingers steady when she took a cigarette from a silver box.

Sergeant Tansill said gently, "I'm afraid there isn't very much you can help us with, Miss Devlin, but I'd like to get a few things straight. The nurse was here attending Miss Thall?"

"Yes. She'd been here since Friday morning."

"Any idea what time she went out last night?"

"I'm afraid not." She lifted gray eyes. "I went out myself, there was something I wanted at the drug store."

"She was gone when you got back?"

"I don't know. I went right to bed when I got in."

Sergeant Tansill asked what time she had gone out and when she had returned, kept his face politely expressionless when Simon Halliday's name was mentioned. He said musingly, "Miss Corey could have left the house any time from eight-thirty on. Didn't go very far, just up over the hill and down to the shore . . . Don't you think it's odd that a nurse would leave her patient alone without letting anyone know, Miss Devlin?"

Sergeant Tansill's eyes were sharp. They didn't miss the pulse that began to stir violently in the girl's white throat just above smooth black wool. "Yes," said Victoria Devlin coolly and without hesitation. "Yes, I do. I can only presume that Nurse Corey must have seen or heard something that alarmed her, and gone out to investigate."

"What's the matter with Miss Thall, anyway?"

"A very bad case of flu, and nerves, I gather." There was a small pause. "She'd had a cold, and then she got drenched in that rainstorm on Thursday. And she'd been doing too much, exhausting herself—she's going to be married in a few weeks and I suppose she was trying to get everything ready."

Sergeant Tansill nodded with complete understanding, as though he himself had once been a flustered bride-to-be. "I'll just have a word with her," he said, moving briskly toward the door. "The nurse may have told her she was going out."

"I'm afraid you can't do that."

The sergeant regarded Victoria with mild astonishment. "I'm afraid I must," he said. "Miss Thall's got flu and nerves. Nurse Corey has rigor mortis."

He had taken another step when the clear voice behind him, appallingly calm, said, "But Miss Thall isn't here, Sergeant."

Sergeant Thall turned slowly. His widening round

brown eyes continued to stare at Victoria Devlin, but he was obviously addressing himself. "Now, how do you like that?" asked Sergeant Tansill softly.

It was much later when Victoria closed the front door behind the sergeant and went slowly across the hall and up the stairs to the third floor sickroom. There hadn't been much time in that half-numb interval after they had entered the house and she had left Sergeant Tansill so hastily on the pretext of illness. But she had used the flying minutes with desperate speed—flinging back the candlewick spread, rumpling the smooth white sheets, denting the pillow. She had thrown a robe of Lilac's over the end of the bed and a pair of white velvet slippers on the floor beside it, placed a water glass from the bathroom on the night table. As a final touch she had pulled open the closet door and disarranged the immaculately neat dressing-table top, as though someone had used comb and powder with careless haste.

As though Lilac Thall, alarmed at either the continued absence of the nurse or the suspected presence of someone else outside the house, had left her lonely third-floor room in a panic. It was the best she could do.

Miraculously, and for the time being, it seemed to have worked. Sergeant Tansill had taken a swift comprehensive look around the room, had gone at once to the closet, had wanted to know without much hope if Victoria could tell him what was missing. After a second's hesitation, she had shaken her head regretfully. Better not describe the cinnamon tweeds Lilac had been wearing. . . . "I'm afraid not, Sergeant. I hadn't seen Lilac in some time. I'm only here on a chance visit as it is—and then, when I saw that Nurse Corey had her hands full, I thought I might be able to help out for a day or two. . . ."

The phone, after that. The swift routine inquiry at the Halliday and Spencer houses. The description of Lilac— "missing since last night or early this morning." The strangely contagious grimness of Sergeant Tansill, in spite of what she knew.

More questions, in the living room.

"When did you last see Miss Thall, Miss Devlin?"

Possible perjury—careful here. "I didn't actually see her, Sergeant. Nurse Corey didn't let me do more than call through the door."

She couldn't retreat, had to go on fostering the illusion. It would give Lilac, wherever she was, a chance to marshall her defenses and explanations. "She was still quite feverish yesterday, and under a mild sedative a lot of the time...."

That was a mistake; she regretted it the moment it was out. Because Sergeant Tansill repeated thoughtfully, "Sedatives ..." and she knew he was thinking of the preceding Wednesday afternoon when Lilac had been found senseless in her car. She said, sliding past it, "I suppose it's possible that she wasn't quite—herself?"

The sergeant went on staring preoccupiedly at the rug, rose at last and asked without a great deal of hope where the garden tools were kept. "It's a routine check—there's just the chance that Fowler chooses his weapon on the scene. This way?"

They were standing outside the front door. Victoria indicated the path around the corner of the house and went back into the library. She was totally unprepared for the half-hour that followed.

Sergeant Tansill was back almost instantly, his face grimly jubilant. He used the phone twice—once to call Millicent Spencer, again to talk rapidly to someone at the police station. When a mysterious fingerprinting ritual had been completed at the shed door he stood motionless in the dripping white mist and appeared to notice Victoria for the first time.

He said soberly, "It isn't much—there's still no weapon. But we know from Mrs. Spencer that there was a sickle bought a few months ago, when Miss Thall had the grounds put in order. It isn't here now. The shed wasn't locked, and the doorknobs got a nice polishing job from somebody—inside and out."

A killer in the shed, separated from her only by the door that led into the living room; Victoria was suddenly made of ice. She said stupidly, "But gardeners wear those heavy gloves—"

"They don't generally steal the tools provided for them," Sergeant Tansill said flatly. "At least Ben Stevens, who did this particular work for Miss Thall, doesn't. He's a native, and he's done gardening here for over forty years—I know him well. The thing is ..." he had forgotten Victoria again, was staring past her shoulder at the grim thing in his own mind; "... have we one weapon or two?

Did Fowler come here by blind chance when he first reached the mainland and maybe think later, after the other two killings, that he'd been seen by someone in this house—the nurse? She wasn't here then, of course, but he couldn't know that if he saw her up on the hill last night. . . ."

He came back out of preoccupation, his brown eyes rounding again out of narrowed thought. "I don't think you'll be in any danger here, Miss Devlin—he's done what he came for and in any case I'll have a man out here as soon after dark as I can. I'm presuming that you'll be around a day or two—until we locate Miss Thall, at any rate."

"Oh, yes," Victoria said steadily. "Yes, I'll be here."

Because she had to stay. In spite of fear and shock and a new distrust of the great empty house around her, she had to be here when hunted, secretive Lilac came back.

She had been standing too long in the third-floor room, staring out the window with its crisp skirts of blue and white. There wasn't much to see in the thick milky blur of fog. The hill behind the house humped dimly up through it, wintry green-brown, its outline broken by a stunted evergreen, a few thorny shrubs, a jagged huddle of rocks.

Nurse Corey, who such a bewilderingly short time ago had been a voice and a pair of competent hands and a brisk, starchy presence, had walked over that hill and down the other side toward the narrow line of stony shore and dark washing water. More than halfway down the hill was a coppice of beeches, crowding against the stone wall that bounded a dead-end lane on one side. That was where the man with the sickle had met her, that was where she lay, stained and slashed, with soggy leaves caught mockingly in her disordered graying hair.

But she had left the house, Victoria thought, on an errand that had to do with Lilac. That was why she had wanted Simon and Victoria to leave first, that was what her tone and bearing had said as she stood in the kitchen doorway last night suggesting the sandalwood soap. Because, earlier, the phone had rung, and it had been Nurse Corey who answered it.

Coincidence, shocking and tragic coincidence had brought the man with the sickle wandering along behind the hill at just that moment last night. It had to be coincidence. William Fowler, the escaped patient from Belle-marsh Sanitarium, could have no connection with Lilac.

Or . . . Suppose she, Victoria, had answered the phone last night? Would there have been a man's voice, cunning, urgent: "I have a message from Lilac. She wants you to meet her behind the hill at . . ."

But that would mean he would know that Lilac wasn't there, the killer who was only a name and a commonplace description and a curved and deadly sickle. No, because then it came back to Lilac, and it mustn't. Yet—where was Lilac? If only she would come! She had said Sunday—and it was now Monday afternoon and Nurse Corey was dead and she, Victoria, had lied to the police. She had lied about Lilac and lied again about not knowing whether Nurse Corey was in the house last night when she got in. She had known, coldly, frightenedly, until she fell into a tossing sleep, that the nurse wasn't there. She had to see Lilac, talk to her, before the police did. . . .

The phone was ringing. Victoria ran down the stairs.

There was no official bulletin that day, but rumor and vague terrors and sudden silences produced their own report.

Missing: Lilac Thall, twenty-six, dark hair, fair complexion, gray eyes, about 5'6". Believed ill, perhaps delirious. Since late Sunday night or early Monday morning.

Missing: William Fowler, thirty-three, committed to Bellemarsh Sanitarium in August, escaped November 13th. Brown hair, fair complexion, blue eyes, about 5'10". Pleasant-mannered, soft-spoken, easily roused to rage. Armed.

Missing: one sickle. . . .

Seacastle huddled into itself, prepared for a state of siege. Schoolrooms were empty, there were no children playing in the streets. Doors were locked, telephones were busy, citizens were deputized and held a solemn conference in Oddfellows' Hall. Seacastle's Chief of Police closeted himself with the state police. There were the usual misleading phone calls full of misinformation, received by Patrolman Peters, who took them all in excited good faith and was consequently brought to the brink of hysteria. Lilac Thall had been seen in a cove along Water Street, babbling in delirium; she had run through a grove near Longmeadow Street with a man with a sickle in hot pursuit; she had been overheard buying a ticket to Boston at the Seacastle station.

A furtive man with a shiny weapon was apprehended on a small private wharf at the end of town. This was the first selectman, cutting fishing line.

The fear penetrated as thoroughly and smotheringly as the fog.

"Gone?" echoed Lilac's sister Millicent blankly at the other end of the phone. "What do you mean, gone? Gone where?"

Victoria set her teeth. It was hardly fair, under the circumstances, to be impatient with Millicent. "Nobody knows where, yet. But there's nothing to worry about. The police—"

"Police! Nobody can tell me," said Millicent passionately, "that Lilac had anything to do with that dreadful thing. Even if she did run away. She must have had a good reason, she must have . . . well, I don't know, but *something* . . ."

"Of course, Millicent," said Victoria.

Millicent hadn't changed, she thought, murmuring soothing things into the phone. She was still blindly protective, still rushing to dire conclusions, still holding a magnifying glass over everything that had to do with Lilac. Simon Halliday had said he didn't want Millicent to know the whole of what had happened to Lilac in her car on Wednesday; with good reason—Millicent would have been stopping startled strangers on the street to say defiantly, "Lilac doesn't take drugs, no matter what they say. . . ."

The indignant surge of sound in Victoria's ear stopped. Millicent said implacably, "I'm coming over," and clicked crisply off the line.

Victoria put the receiver back and went on looking at mist peering whitely in at the windows. Hard to believe that that same voice had dropped to an angry contemptuous whisper last night outside the Cabot House. 'You stupid fool . . . I told you you wouldn't be able to get in to see her.' Freddy Spencer had tried, then, and Nurse Corey had made her last formidable refusal. Would Sergeant Tansill, wondered Victoria, get around to the Spencers in his effort to find out more accurately when Nurse Corey had been killed? .

Of course not. The protective reassurances came blanketing back again. It has nothing to do with Lilac, with any of us. It might have been a total stranger who was killed; one dizzyingly fractional chance made it be Nurse Corey instead.

Messages for Lilac ... idiocy to write them down, but it might look odd if there were no record at all of the calls and visits of the past two days. And there was nothing to do now in any case but wait—for word from Lilac, for the avalanche of questions that was building up on all sides. Olive Stacey, Simon Halliday's cousin, had said after a stunned second of shock when Sergeant Tansill had called to inquire curtly if Lilac was there, that she would be over as soon as possible, to see if she could be of any help. *Help*, thought Victoria ironically, and began to write.

Around her the mist-wrapped house was still and empty. There was the droning tick of the grandfather clock and the little blurry lipping sounds of the water behind the hill, but they had become a familiar part of the silence. "Saturday," wrote Victoria. "Millicent phoned, later brought jelly." (Lilac had said, with a pale tight smile, "Millicent will bring jelly, it's her way of meeting crises.") What else had there been? "Simon phoned. His aunt sent flowers. Rufe came. A Mrs. Gilling"—or had it been Gilman, or Tillingham, and what difference did it make anyway—"phoned to invite you to dinner.

"Sunday." The pen ran scratchily dry; Victoria filled it and lighted a cigarette, listened to the silence for a moment and wrote, "Olive Stacey brought books." And nearly penetrated to the third floor sickroom, she thought, and got turned away by Nurse Corey just in time.

Someone else had called on Sunday morning, a man who had asked for Lilac and had then hung up abruptly without identifying himself. Skip him; "Rufe sent flowers. Simon came over. . . ."

And Monday, said the ironic and unwritten words, Lilac's absence discovered, Nurse Corey's body found, Lilac's description taken by the police.

The doorbell made her start.

Olive Stacey stepped in out of the mist, closing the heavy front door behind her. She was a tall woman in her early thirties, with a face that reminded Victoria of a tawny, amiable cat: narrow cheeks and pointed chin, quirked feathery brows over slightly tilted eyes, amber hair pulled back carelessly, so that there were straying locks and tendrils. Victoria had remembered her only vaguely, knew that she was a distant relative of the Hallidays who had become, ten or twelve years ago, an integral part of the family.

She followed Victoria into the living room now, fumbling absently at her gloves. "No word from Lilac, I suppose? No news at all?"

"Not yet."

Olive sat down, frowning anxiously, on one end of the sofa. She said slowly, "I can't understand it. She knew, we all knew it wasn't a good idea to go wandering about alone at night with that—that lunatic around; we were talking about it only the other day. Unless she tried . . ." she gave a final tug at yellow pigskin and looked grimly at her lap. "She might have thought she could help the nurse. But still . . ."

Her hands were free; she flexed them a little. Victoria saw that the knuckles of the short blunt fingers were slightly swollen and twisted. Olive caught the fleeting glance, and looked down and said absently, "Arthritis. It always seems to get worse in this weather. . . . You'd think the police would have gotten somewhere by now, formed some definite theory. . . ."

"I suppose they're doing everything they can. Lilac may have gone out and been frightened, and be hiding somewhere," said Victoria unconvincingly, and thought with a spurt of resentment, This is frightful. All these people exposed to needless worry . . . where *is* she?

"Rufe's spent hours with the police already. Simon is frantic, of course," said Olive, lighting a cigarette. "He and Freddy—Freddy works at Simon's agency, you know—are coming right out. I suppose they could help if there's a search. . . ." Her voice trailed away. She made an aimless gesture with the hand that held the cigarette, and the steady thread of blue smoke dissolved in a thin flurry.

She said softly, almost to herself, "I wonder when Lilac was last in this house?"

Silence. Dimly, the clock and the faraway swish of the water. Victoria sat like a statue, her face blank and polite and wondering, and Olive flicked ash from her cigarette and said in a troubled voice, "I have the oddest impression now that she wasn't here, but of course I didn't think anything of it at the time."

"I don't—what do you mean?" It was difficult for Victoria to get the words out.

Olive looked up. She said, "I mean Sunday—last night—when she telephoned."

CHAPTER 4

"Telephoned? Oh, then Lilac—" *Careful.* She had almost said, "Lilac told you herself." Victoria caught it back with the secrecy that had become instinct in this house, and finished, "Then Lilac was all right as late as that. At least— did she sound like herself?"

That had been dangerously close—too close. For just an instant Victoria had an idea that Olive's brown gaze had turned exploring, that the other woman was waiting for something more. The impression passed, but she had had time to think warily, Not yet. There may be a reason for Lilac's coming back like this. Have it out with her later, not with people whom she didn't trust before.

"There's so little to tell," Olive was saying hesitantly, and then went on to describe the phone call that was, aside from the fact of its having occurred at all, curiously meaningless. Victoria listened and tried to reason through a fog of mystification.

At some time close to ten o'clock on the preceding evening, Olive said, Lilac had telephoned and asked to speak to Simon. As she had thought she heard Simon's car pulling into the driveway just then, Olive had told Lilac to wait just a moment while she went to get him. Lilac had said, however, not to bother, and had hung up. "I thought," said Olive, puckering her brows, "that she might mean to call back in a few minutes, but she didn't. And it wasn't Simon after all, or if it was he didn't come into the house right away. So I left a message and went on up to bed. Of course, if I'd known then . . ."

So Lilac, after planning and contriving and drawing Victoria and the murdered nurse into her desperately secret scheme, had walked boldly up to put her head in the lion's mouth.

Ten minutes later, Victoria went to the door with Olive. The mist still hung, swallowing the damp green-brown lawn and banking itself in a wet silvery huddle in the angle of the fence.

"Lilac sounded rather—odd," Olive said abruptly, pulling on her gloves. "Rather as though—you knew, didn't you, that she'd been found in her car last week in a very peculiar condition?"

The wet rhododendrons at the doorway glistened and dripped. Drugs—again. Lilac's clean black-and-whiteness suddenly blurred and stumbling and ugly . . . Victoria knew what Olive was going to say even before the puzzled, reluctant words came out.

"She sounded a little like . . . that," said Olive without meeting Victoria's eyes, and disappeared into the mist.

Portrait of Lilac—new, strange, as shocking as though a painted canvas had begun to ripple and stir and grow alien features. Millicent Spencer, Lilac's sister, was shortly to add another brush-stroke to it.

She arrived in tears, a small, pink, carefully groomed woman who somehow contrived to look gently dewy and pitiful instead of wet and wretched. Victoria, acutely uncomfortable in the face of her sisterly grief, found sherry and words of reassurance, and, when they were in the living room again, watched Millicent studying herself critically in her compact mirror and marvelled that she could be Lilac's sister at all. To realize that they had had the same parents was like being told that a master etcher had also turned his hand to a fruity, rainbowed still-life. Where Lilac's face had sting and gaiety, Millicent's was full of immaculately powdered serenity; where Lilac had fine polished edges, Millicent was only a feminine blur. And yet there was a strong bond between them, with Millicent more passionately protective than the mother who had died five years ago.

"Poor Nurse Corey," Millicent was saying perfunctorily. "Think of it—Lilac's own sickle! I nearly fainted when that policeman called, but I remember quite well when Lilac bought it for what's-his-name, the gardener." She snapped her compact shut. "Of course, it was odd that Nurse Corey should have left the house while you were out, with Lilac so sick. It was awfully unprofessional, don't you think?"

Victoria observed dryly that it had also been very unfortunate.

"Oh, of course. Poor thing." Millicent shuddered. "That man, that Fowler creature—isn't it shocking to know that he's still at large? Why, I really felt nervous even coming out today. And when you think that Lilac . . ."

"Now, Millicent . . ." Victoria shook off a sudden cold vision of blackness behind the hill, of water splashing icily against the shore, of Nurse Corey's rubber-soled tread carrying her briskly to her death. She said abruptly, "By the way, what time were you and Freddy here last night? Nurse Corey was still in then, I suppose?"

Millicent's eyes widened. She picked up her bag and gloves and said with faint surprise, "Last night? Oh, but we weren't, Victoria. Nurse Corey had said no one could see Lilac until today, don't you remember?"

Millicent was lying, and lying very well, too, with eyes like flowers under the smooth lift of her brows. It didn't matter, apart from the oddness of her bothering to lie at all. It was when she was at the door, smoothing brown suède over her fluttery hands and looking curiously about her, that Millicent added her small jolting touch to the alien portrait of Lilac.

"What lovely asters. Did the Hallidays send them? I suppose Simon's worried to death . . . I wonder if anyone's thought of asking Charles Storrow if he knows anything about all this."

"Charles Storrow?" The name was vaguely familiar.

Millicent nodded, her eyes bright. "He's always thought the world of Lilac, you know—and she saw him only last week." She caught her breath. "Not that there's anything between them," she said defensively. "Heavens, I didn't mean that. Lilac's the last girl in the world who'd wear one man's ring and have an affair with another one. She did see that he was asked to luncheon last week with all of us, but that was only to be kind. . . ."

Victoria had stopped listening. She thought numbly, Millicent protecting Lilac all those years, being buffer between her erring younger sister and outraged authority. . . . The time Lilac was caught exchanging torrid notes with a Harvard sophomore. The time Lilac was discovered to be cutting a good two-thirds of all her classes at Miss Harvey's. The time Lilac pawned the miniature of her grandmother to buy a ouija board . . .

And all the other occasions when parental wrath was softened and punishment lightened because gentle Millicent had pleaded and implored. And no one had ever wondered how Lilac had been found out in the first place.

Victoria thought in chilled amazement, How could we all have been so blind for so long? Millicent hates Lilac, and always has.

Go back, then. Go back, because somehow, at some time during her strange visit to Victoria's apartment in New York, Lilac must have given herself away.

Thursday. It had rained that night, furring the reflections in the streets, spitting at her apartment windows in sudden rustling gusts. It was a good night to go to bed early with cigarettes and a book and Victoria had done just that, so that she had to catch up her robe and slide bare feet into slippers when the buzzer sounded.

The lobby telephone didn't work. She had heard the elevator doors close by the time she hooked the chain on the door and opened it to look out on a slit of tiny tiled hall. And there, incredibly, stood Lilac Thall, whom she hadn't seen in over a year.

Lilac's cinnamon tweeds were wet, and rain made rhinestones in her straight shining dark hair. She hadn't wasted time after her first absent greeting, hadn't seemed to think eleven o'clock was an odd hour for an unannounced call. "Victoria—first of all, are you free this week-end? Or if there's something can you possibly break it?"

That came even before she had stripped off her gloves to let lamplight drown and dazzle in the diamond on her left hand. Her eyes had followed Victoria's. "Oh, yes—I'm engaged. To Simon Halliday—do you remember him? They've had a summer place in Seacastle for years, and now they live there permanently. You've met them—if not Simon his brother Rufe, anyway. We're going to be married in a little less than a month, and I've got to be away for a few days before that without—without anyone knowing. I've got to, Victoria, and I can't unless you'll help me. . . ."

The plan came tumbling out then. Victoria had made coffee in the little kitchen while Lilac perched on the table, her narrow face pale and taut with pleading. "It's only a week-end, and no harm done—except that I must be away. Can't you trust me, Victoria? Just for three days?"

Victoria had been reluctant and more than a little impatient. "It isn't a matter of trust, Lilac, and you know it perfectly well. It won't work, that's all. People don't walk around hale and hearty one day and get hovered over by a private nurse the next. And if you refuse to see anybody at all, it's just asking for trouble. Someone's bound to produce another doctor—"

"Nurse Corey will take care of that. And you can say you've seen me. Oh God, Victoria, you've got to. Don't you see? There's no one else I can turn to, no one—and I must get away. I'll be there myself to explain things on Monday, so you needn't have anything to do with that part of it."

"Suppose," Victoria was matter-of-fact, curling into an armchair with her slippered feet tucked up, "someone penetrates this inner sanctum? What happens then?"

She was shocked at the result of the idle, necessary question. The flesh tones died out of Lilac's face, leaving it tallowy and tight, as though the skin were stretched too bindingly over the bold handsome bone structure beneath. "No one must," said Lilac in a voice that was no more than a whisper. "If anyone found out, I think I'd—" Her hands went sharply, blindly together.

It was then that Victoria agreed to the deception. Reluctantly still, and against her better judgment, but unavoidably because Lilac had come to her in fear and trust and desperation, and there was nothing else she could do. She remembered now the rain slatting against the windows, the silence and cigarette blueness and coffee fragrance in the apartment, the feeling of small-hours exhaustion although it wasn't quite midnight.

She remembered Lilac, too, limp and drained with relief, putting on the dark brilliant lipstick she always wore and refusing the offer of Victoria's couch. "Thanks, but I—I've a hotel room." She hadn't; Victoria had recognized evasion even then, but Lilac was growing restless and subduedly eager now that her way was clear. "I'll be back Sunday night at the latest. I won't try to thank you, Victoria, but you'll never know . . ."

No, there was no clue.

Lilac's last words, "You'll never know . . ." had a bleak finality now that hadn't been intended on Thursday night. Victoria, who found to her astonishment that she had made and swallowed a cup of tea, began to rinse dishes at the sink, her hands mechanically busy, her mind hopefully idle. And all at once there was something else, stirred up out of her joggled memory.

It was a rainy day, years ago, and Lilac and she had been driving up to Seacastle. When they stopped at a diner for coffee, Lilac had slammed the car door, leaving her key in the ignition. Her voice after the first appalled shock, had been rueful: "Oh, damn. *Damn.* If I'd only taken Rufe Halliday's advice and strapped another key on the underside of the car . . . oh well, come on, let's find a garage."

Words out of the past, but still . . . Swiftly, not knowing quite what it would prove, Victoria opened the back door and ran through mist to the garage. It wasn't locked. Lilac's blue convertible stood in dimness, surrounded by a chilly aura of gasoline and metal and damp brick and concrete.

She found it almost at once, the strip of adhesive tape with the faint outline of a car key showing through, on the undercurve of the right rear fender. The tape was immaculately snowy, although the arching metal around it was ridged and crusted with dried mud. Victoria rose slowly to her feet and went out into the blurry silver fog again. Someone had replaced the tape very recently indeed—after Wednesday's storm, after Thursday's continuing rain. Lilac herself had said she had stayed close to the house on Thursday, as part of her developing plan.

Lilac had used the car and replaced the key, of course—and yet that was shriekingly wrong, and temptingly open to argument when you considered that anyone close to her would have known where to find another key. Another key . . . the brown calf handbag brushed disturbingly against Victoria's consciousness. It had been in the house yesterday, lying casually on some appropriate surface. She couldn't remember having seen it since. Half-idly, with the house silent and gray around her, she began to search.

She wasn't left long to her errand. The doorbell rang and Victoria, suddenly aware of dust along the hem of her dress and a streak of oil on one wrist, went to the hall to let in Simon Halliday and a man whom he introduced absently as Millicent's husband, Freddy Spencer.

This was the man behind the voice that had said so softly and cuttingly, "You're in this just as deep as I am, Millie. . . ." But it was difficult to imagine anything approaching menace in connection with Freddy Spencer. He looked to be the most innocuous of men, the most obedient of husbands, Victoria thought: round beguiling face, smooth sandy head, light eyes that held an air of solicitous concern and an anxiety to be liked. In his late thirties, he had already managed to accumulate a modestly portly silhouette.

"No news?" Simon asked abruptly. "But there wouldn't be, of course. We stopped at the police station on the way out from Boston. I don't suppose you've found anything here in the house that would . . ."

"I'm afraid not." She had been unmoved by Millicent's tears; at the look of desperate calm in Simon's face Victoria felt guilt and a fresh wave of anger at the ill-conceived plan that had put them all here.

"Now, Simon, old fellow, the police . . ." Freddy Spencer began soothingly, but Simon had stopped in his long slouching stride to jerk his head up and look at Victoria. "Did she take a bag?"

"Not that I know of."

Curiously enough, Lilac hadn't had any kind of luggage with her; the knowledge, examined for the first time, sent apprehension through Victoria. Lilac had expected to be away for only three days, at a hotel probably, where they would launder her blouse and press her suit. But the time was drawing out, and it meant that somewhere Lilac's plans had gone askew.

"No car, no bag." Simon was staring at the rug, bright gray eyes narrowed and fierce, as though the answer were locked somewhere among twisted Persian trees in flame and gold and blue. "If she went of her own accord, she can't have gone far. If she didn't, they'd have found some . . . trace."

"Maybe's she's hiding," said Freddy Spencer mildly.

The words were idle, and Victoria's quick startled glance told her that he had said them at random and without conviction. But Simon had swung to stare at him scathingly. "Hiding? What for—fun and games? She was fond of Nurse Corey, she'd have gotten in touch—" he broke off at the sound of voices on the path outside. "Here's Rufe, and Aunt Grace."

Gathering of the clan—and a swift probing inspection from two more pairs of eyes: Rufus Halliday's gray and dark-lashed, startlingly like Simon's, and his aunt's warm mahogany brown, alert and noticing in spite of instant, automatic charm.

Victoria had remembered Rufe from one far-off summer in Seacastle, had been shocked when she met him again on Saturday at his white worried face, at the nervous movements of hands he didn't seem to know what to do with. He looked calmer now and almost cheerful, as though some inner resolve had stiffened him and he had taken on the burden of optimism for the entire Halliday household.

He said, taking her hand, "You look knocked out by all this, Victoria. We'll give Lilac the devil when she gets back. By the way, have you met Aunt Grace . . . ?"

Grace Halliday must have been in her early fifties; she looked, thought Victoria, like a miraculous forty. Her still-dark hair was swept up and away from a faintly haughty but charming face; her quick smile of pleasure might have been the result of a pressed button labeled Delight. "Miss Devlin. We've talked on the phone, of course, but it's so nice to meet you. And how lucky we all are that Lilac has such a devoted friend. . . ." Another button: Gravity. "This is a frightful time for all of us, and we do appreciate your being here though it's quite selfish of us, I know. This ghastly business about the sickle . . . The police say they expect word of Lilac at any moment, but that's always so inconclusive, isn't it?"

"A note," said Simon suddenly in the background. "Do you think she might have left some sort of indication . . . ?"

The search began, then, the half-aimless, conscientious prowling of people who know they will find nothing but feel obliged to leave no stone unturned. Victoria noticed to her surprise that Grace Halliday's left hand was artificial, a cleverly manipulated thing of plastic and flesh-toned leather. She hadn't meant to stare, and she started guiltily when Rufe Halliday's voice at her elbow said, "She lost it ten years ago, in the same train wreck that killed her husband."

"Oh. Heavens, was I—"

"No, but you can't help seeing it." They were away from the others, and Rufe looked directly at her, his face troubled. "Be honest, Victoria. Do you think something's happened to Lilac?"

"No." She had said it with too much violence, and she tried instantly to modify it. "This—disappearance may have nothing to do with Fowler or Nurse Corey at all. Something might have come up—"

"What, Victoria?"

His voice, soft and almost coaxing, put her instantly on guard. It was dangerous to talk to Rufe, whose impersonal kind of gentleness could trap you into the truth. Victoria said crisply, "I've no idea. I suppose someone's looked on the windowseat in the hall . . . ?"

Outside, the blind gray mist turned to darkness. Freddy Spencer departed, murmuring apologies about Millicent's being alarmed. Victoria, who had pretended to search for a note, realized with a queer sharp uneasiness that the brown calf handbag, where Lilac had said she would leave her keys, was gone.

"Won't you change your mind, Miss Devlin, and spend the night with us? There's plenty of room, and we'd be delighted to have you." Grace Halliday, buttoning beautiful tweeds at her slender throat, smiled at Victoria with an air of concern. "I don't like to think of your being here alone, under the circumstances."

"Why don't you, Victoria?" said Rufe. "There's nothing you can do here, after all."

They were persuasive, even Simon, who came up just then, let his eyes rest briefly on Victoria, and said, "Good idea. You'll hear whatever there is to hear just as quickly at our house—why don't you get your toothbrush and come along?"

Were they anxious beyond the bounds of courtesy to get her out of this house? But that was nonsense; worry and the approach of real alarm, stemming from her own guilty knowledge, had made her hypersensitive. The prospect of companionship during the long grim evening ahead was tempting, but Victoria was firm with her refusal and thanks. She had lied to all of them and, most important, to the police; she had to talk to Lilac before anyone else could, so that they could cement some sort of believable tale. She said, "It's awfully kind of you, but they're sending a policeman later on and I think I'd better stay. . . ."

And in the end they went, taking the reassuring stir and presence and sound of voices with them. Simon turned to look back at her, the overhead light slanting across his sharply contoured face and noncommittal eyes. He said, "Give us a ring if you change your mind. I could be over here to pick you up in two shakes," and Victoria, closing and locking the door behind them, knew that he had sensed her cloaked nervousness, and felt a little less desolate.

What now? It was only a little after six, too early for the dinner she didn't want. The windows were dark and shining between folds of flowered linen, the living room a long silent cave of color. Nothing to do now but wait for the library phone to come to life. Victoria crossed to the bookcase beside the fireplace, chose a volume at random and sat down in the pale yellow corduroy wing chair.

The library clock ticked, a tiny italics to silence. Beyond the hill, the harbor wove and hissed on the shore, the last sound Nurse Corey must have heard in ebbing, agonized consciousness. Fiercely, Victoria turned a page.

The house was stuffy, the air close around her. There had been too many people here, smoking too many cigarettes; Victoria made an involuntary movement to rise and sat rigidly back. It wasn't safe to go outside at night, or even to open a door or a window on blackness. Nurse Corey had walked up over the hill after dark, and hadn't come back.

Last night there had been a killer roaming outside this house.

Her throat was dry. A glass of water, she thought mechanically, and put her cigarette in the ashtray and looked up and saw the hand at the window.

CHAPTER 5

THE hand itself was gloved; it was the narrow strip of pale wrist that had caught her eye. For a second the spread fingers balanced delicately against the pane, and then above it showed the dim blot of a man's face, peering whitely between the curtains.

William Fowler. It was all her brain could produce under shock and hypnosis. Armed. Dangerous.

Victoria sat frozen in the wing chair, her nails biting into yellow corduroy, her heartbeats roaring in her ears. *Run,* screamed her nerves in soundless panic, run, get to the phone, the police. The front door— Oh, God ... locked or not?

And the kitchen door, unlocked.

Release came so suddenly that she was on her feet, swaying; the next instant she had raced through the hall and into the kitchen and was fumbling with the bolt on the back door. When it went home she braced herself for a moment against the wooden panels, waiting for the trembling limpness to pass. As she stood there, the doorbell rang.

I might have opened it, thought Victoria, sick and appalled; if I hadn't seen him at the window I would have opened the door and let him in. . . . The phone. She could call from the second-floor extension; the policeman might be on his way here now. The front door was locked. She remembered now the click of the mechanism under her fingers when she had closed the door on the Hallidays and safety.

Someone was calling. Halfway across the hall toward the stairs, Victoria paused in nightmare and listened. It was a man's voice, muffled and urgent. ". . . come in for a minute? It's Storrow, Charles Storrow—"

It might be. And it might be William Fowler, plausible and persuasive until his killing rage took possession of him. Victoria's fingers uncurled stiffly at her sides and indecision went. She advanced silently toward the door, snapped off the hall light, turned on the outside lamp. After a slanting glance through one of the narrow recessed windows she felt, almost tangibly, the ebb of fear. The man who stood on damp flagstones under the sudden shower of light was six feet tall or more—well over the 5'10" of the official description—and the crest of hair over a thin drawn face was a brilliant paint-pot red. As she watched, his arm came up as though he were going to ring again, and Victoria swung the door open.

The man stepped into the hall, blinking and uncertain in the dim light. He was in his late twenties; tight anxious lines around his mouth and eyes made him look younger. He stripped off black leather driving gloves and said apologetically, "I'm sorry if I frightened you. I shouldn't have looked through the window like that, but there were people here before and I didn't know whether you were alone. . . . I'm Charles Storrow, a friend of Lilac's."

He had been waiting outside in the dark then—how long? Victoria, still weak with relief, introduced herself and waited. Storrow didn't take off his trench coat. He said, "May I?" and dropped into a chair, long bony hands playing nervously along its arms, gray eyes worried: "I suppose there's no news yet about Lilac?"

"No." Was his reason for standing at the window as simple and frank as it sounded?

"She'd been ill," Charles Storrow said slowly, "or—supposed to be. That's why I didn't know whether or not I ought to tell the police about her coming to see me yesterday. It might look . . . anyway, you're a friend of hers and I thought maybe you might know what I ought to do."

The shakiness of reaction was swept out of Victoria.

She stared, her face blank, her voice incredulous. "Lilac—went to see you?"

"Yes. Well, nearly." He had hunched himself forward in the chair, looking at her with a mixture of eagerness and perplexity. "Yesterday at a little after five, it must have been, because it was getting on for dusk . . ."

And Victoria, listening over a cold inner fear, heard it come back again to the car and the pink and gold kerchief.

At a little after five on Sunday afternoon, Charles Storrow said, he had been weatherstripping the windows of the small house on Blackfan Road where he lived alone, when he heard a car's horn outside. By the time he got to the front windows, the car had turned around—it was a dead-end road—and Lilac had waved at him and driven off before he had a chance to do more than open the door.

"Mightn't it," said Victoria carefully, "have been someone else, in Lilac's car?"

Charles Storrow shook his red head. "How could it have been? She had a pink thing that I recognized over her hair . . . and there's that funny way she has of waving, with a cigarette. Besides," the last trace of doubt went out of his voice, "there are only a couple of other houses on that street, and I'm at the end. Why would anyone else drive out there and sound the horn? That's another thing she does. I keep telling her it's rude and she goes right on—"

He broke off, a dark flush flooding up to his hairline, and Victoria dropped her lashes over a look of pity. With Lilac's wedding less than a month away, Charles Storrow was still deeply and wretchedly in love with her, and was denied even the scant comfort of being able to show his frantic worry openly.

"So you see," said Storrow, "I don't know whether I ought to go to the police about this or not. I got a very cold reception at lunch last week," he grinned a little, bitterly, "from the aunt—Mrs. Halliday. And I don't want her twisting things about, taking it out on Lilac. What's more, I don't trust any of that bunch."

"Why?"

Charles Storrow stood up, slapping the black gloves against the side of his coat. "I heard about what happened to Lilac after that lunch," he said quietly. "I don't know which of them, or why, but I do know that one of them drugged her."

Victoria went with him to the door. She said that,

having seen Lilac's car himself on Sunday afternoon, Simon Halliday would undoubtedly inform the police, removing the onus from Storrow. Locking the door behind him, going mechanically to the kitchen to start dinner, she went back over what he had told her.

'That funny way she has of waving, with a cigarette.' And Simon Halliday had said, 'I know the way Lilac drives.' The intangibles, more clinching than the car and the pink and gold kerchief, noticed by the two men who loved Lilac.

Might as well admit it. Lilac had apparently come back to Seacastle after all—and had disappeared cleanly, without a trace.

Sergeant Tansill had sat late in the police station on High Street. There was the autopsy report on Nurse Corey, and the bulletins on the missing Lilac Thall and the escaped William Fowler to wait for. Across from him, riding in lazy half-circles in a creaking swivel chair, the coroner smoked a cigar that smelled like a clambake, and chatted.

"Now you take a sickle," said the coroner meditatively. "Not a very handy thing to kill people with, you know. Do better to stick to a good old-fashioned bread knife."

"He likes sickles," Sergeant Tansill said moodily. "Do you have to smoke that thing in here?"

"Yes. Tell you what, though, he's getting tired of his technique." The coroner took another creaking spin. "The other two, the Brainard child and the Cossett woman, were stunned first. The nurse wasn't. I suppose there wasn't anything around to do it with."

He stood up, looking at the sergeant, grim and silent behind his desk. "What are the chances on the Thall girl? Think you'll find her?"

"Oh, we'll find her," said Sergeant Tansill harshly, and pushed back his chair with violence. "By tomorrow we'll have the whole state here. And planes and volunteers and divers. Sure, we'll find her—whatever there's left to find."

When the telephone rang at eight-thirty on that Monday evening Victoria was in the living room, the flowered curtains drawn, the radio on to defeat the silence. A large shy policeman had come half an hour earlier. He would be around the Thall grounds or in the neighborhood until daylight, he said. He refused the offer of the living room couch; the Seacastle police force, it seemed, couldn't spare a man for exclusive duty that night. Victoria reached the library before the second ring and listened with the now-familiar feeling of flatness to Simon Halliday's voice.

"Changed your mind about coming here for the night? I wish you would, Victoria."

I can't, thought Victoria, steeling herself and not listening. I can't leave now, when no one knows— "Thank you just the same, but I think I'd better stay. There's a policeman around somewhere—not in the house, but not far away."

"I think you ought to have a dog," said Simon's voice gravely.

"It's a little late to go shopping for a dog, isn't it?"

"One of our Saint Bernards, I mean," Simon said patiently. "We have three, and they've never done an honest day's work in their lives. Would you like me to bring one over?"

A dog, something else living in this vacuum of fog and fear—"Yes, if it isn't a nuisance."

"It isn't. Be there in five minutes," said Simon cheerfully, and hung up.

It was closer to fifteen minutes before he finally knocked. Victoria opened the front door and stared down at a huge dark gold Saint Bernard with a mournful white-blazed face. Simon, at the other end of the leash, said, "This is Shandy," and bent to unsnap the leash and fondle the dog's head. "He's not awfully friendly, but the other two are in their dotage and not much good as watchdogs, I'm afraid."

Shandy, freed, padded sombrely to the door of the living room. Victoria looked after him, smiling. "Thanks very much. I will feel better . . . coffee? Or a drink?"

There wasn't any news, he told her, holding an ice tray under hot water in the kitchen. The usual false alarms—five or six Lilacs and a dozen William Fowlers had been duly traced to their own innocent homes. "The papers will be full of it tomorrow," Simon said; "Soda or water?" and held both glasses briefly under the faucet. In the living room, he lighted Victoria's cigarette and his own and sat back against the couch, passing a tired hand across his eyes. "The newspapers, the radio—they ought to reach her, wherever she is." His mouth looked stubborn, refusing to voice the possibility that Lilac was beyond the realm of sight and sound and would never be reached by anything again.

Victoria, across the brilliant lamplit width of the room, was suddenly aware of him for the first time. Before she had come to Seacastle he had been only a name, a brother of Rufus Halliday, whom she had known for one summer years ago; the man to whom Lilac Thall was engaged. Then for the two and a half days after her arrival he had been the most essential person to be deceived—a relentless visitor with a too-alert pair of eyes. Now, looking at the dark head tilted wearily back against the couch, the sardonic face stripped to helplessness, she thought with a feeling of astonishment, If I loved him I couldn't let him go through this. Not for a week-end, not for an hour. . . .

The dog shifted restlessly at Simon's knee. He dropped his gaze, and Victoria knew confusedly that they had been staring at each other and was glad, five minutes later, when he rose to go. "He's been fed," Simon said, nodding down at the Saint Bernard, who had accompanied them hopefully to the door. "I'll have someone pick him up in the morning if you find he's getting underfoot." With the door open on the dripping November night, he added, "I told Tansill about seeing Lilac's car out yesterday afternoon. There'll probably be someone around to look at it in the morning," and was gone before she could speak.

Half an hour later, with Shandy lured upstairs to the second floor by means of a bowl of milk, Victoria lay in bed in darkness and tried to mesmerize herself to sleep. Wasn't there something about concentrating on a black pinpoint at the end of a long alley . . . you willed it toward you, growing bigger and bigger, and at the moment of impact you were theoretically asleep.

But instead of the black pinpoint there was Lilac slumped at the wheel of the convertible, drugged and helpless.

There was the phone call that had, she was almost sure of it, taken Nurse Corey out of the house and into the path of her killer.

There was something Millicent wanted kept from Lilac, because Lilac would tell Simon. There was the calf bag that had been in the house as late as Sunday, and was now gone . . . and there was the missing sickle. Behind it all flickered the pale frightened face of Lilac Thall.

There was, overwhelmingly, the web of lies concerning Lilac's non-appearance—a tissuey net to begin with, a binding irrevocable thing of steel now that an official search had begun. Should she retract the entire story now and come forward with the truth? Or was Lilac, who had trusted her, praying somewhere for a few more hours of silence?

Victoria lifted her head sharply as a vine scraped the window, and was asleep before it touched the pillow again.

The phone. It was morning in a gray dissolving world of water. Victoria groped her way sleepily into the shadowed hall and picked up the receiver. At the other end of the wire, Millicent Spencer's voice sounded damp and miserable. She was wretched, she said, and Freddy had to be at the Hallidays' to go over some papers with Simon: if she called Freddy there and had him pick her up in the car, would Victoria stay with her for a little while? She'd go out of her mind if she didn't have someone to talk to. . . .

It was impossible to refuse. Victoria said she would be ready in half an hour and was bathed and dressed in under that. The navy gabardine suit made her look like a ghost, she thought, standing in the watery wash of light at the window: pale oval face, pale hair, shadowed eyes no grayer than the rain. Lipstick helped. With the smooth metal case still in her hand she rubbed a clear patch in a misted windowpane and watched rain seething against the house, driven before a northeast wind.

The landscape was bleak and sodden—low iron sky, the blurred hump of the hill, an oilskinned figure twisting along the little lane that skirted the rise and led down to the harbor and the inevitable lobster traps. The northeaster flags would be raised at the old fort at the other end of the town. If any tangible traces of William Fowler had remained in the coppice behind the hill they would now be obliterated. . . .

Freddy Spencer was apologetic about bringing her out into the rain. "I'd have stayed with Millie myself," he swung the wheel to avoid a water-filled hole in the road, "but Simon isn't going into town today and I've got to bring some stuff into the office for him. I tell Lilac," said Freddy with an edged and deprecating laugh, "that we're getting a slave-driver in the family. Here we are—but you've never been here before, have you?"

The Spencers' house, on a hill above the harbor, was small and perfect, its roofline modified Dutch colonial, its shutters faded sapphire against old white clapboards. Inside, even Millicent's overstuffed taste hadn't spoiled the beauty of moldings and mantels and small-paned windows.

Millicent herself was upstairs in bed. Freddy took Victoria to the door, poked his smooth sandy head into the room, said, "Here's Miss Devlin, dear," as though he were a retriever bringing back a particularly fine duck, and was gone. His voice floated up the stairs; "Try not to worry, Millie. I'll call you." The front door closed.

Millicent looked pink and woebegone against piled pillows. Her eyelids were shiny, as though she had been crying, and her usually impeccable dark hair was pushed carelessly away from her face. Victoria, who had been conscious of renewed dislike for Lilac's placid, sweet, traitorous sister, felt a pang. She said, "I'm sorry you aren't well, Millicent. Have you had breakfast?"

Millicent said that she had, but that she would like another cup of coffee; she had hardly slept at all from worry over Lilac, and she thought she was catching a cold. "Better stay in bed then," said Victoria, and escaped to the kitchen.

She had put cups on a tray and was pouring coffee from the percolator on the stove when the phone rang. It sounded as though it had come from the rose and blue living room. Victoria put the percolator down, called, "I'll get it," and went through an arched dining alcove toward the repeated ringing. Millicent was on the stairs, her feet thrust into slippers, her bed-jacket clutched around her. She said rapidly and a little breathlessly, "I'll take it, Victoria, it's probably—" but Victoria had located the phone on a small stand just inside the living room doorway and had the receiver in her hand. Standing there, she could see an incongruous half of Millicent motionless on the stairs; a curving edge of lace, a fold of rumpled nightgown, a hand on the banister. In her ear a man's voice said, "This is Fox, Mrs. Spencer. I want you to tell your—"

"This isn't Mrs. Spencer. If you'll wait just a minute—"

Millicent hadn't moved. She said in an unnaturally high, steady voice, "Who is it?"

Victoria covered the receiver. "A Mr. Fox. Shall I tell him—?"

Millicent's small rose-tipped hand left the banister,

came back again and tightened, the knuckles showing white. "Tell him I'm ill. Tell him I—" the words came in a little rush. "Say that I'll call him back."

If the telephone call had upset her, Millicent showed no sign of it when Victoria went back upstairs with the coffee tray. She was in bed again, her pillows straightened, her dark hair in smooth waves around her face. She was herself once more, calm and sweet and pink—and curious.

"It was so good of you to come, Victoria. I was feeling wretched about Lilac before you got here, but now I feel there's hope, don't you?" Millicent pulled the down comforter higher about her. "Will you be able to stay—but I imagine there are things you have to get back to in New York."

"As a matter of fact, there aren't. I'd left the magazine I was working for anyway, so it's just a matter of looking around. . . . Cream?"

"Heavens, no, I must lose ten pounds," Millicent said. "I'm a sight. No sugar, either, but if you'd hand me my bag, over there on the dresser, I've some saccharine. It makes coffee taste like nothing on earth, but I suppose it *is* thinning. . . ."

Victoria, crossing the room and returning with the black calf bag, thought with a sudden thrust of bleakness that Millicent was right, that it had come now to the point of there being "hope" for Lilac. Not only a matter of time any more, not just a baffling failure to turn up at the promised moment. And was she herself, by not telling the police the truth about Lilac's actions, providing fresh danger for Lilac instead of concealing safety?

Sitting there in the bedroom, watching Millicent tug exasperatedly at the zipper of the black handbag, she didn't think so. After all, unless Simon Halliday and Charles Storrow—and yes, Olive Stacey, who had answered Lilac's phone call on Sunday night—were all badly mistaken in what they thought they had seen and heard, then Lilac was in Seacastle, as the police believed.

And what, in essence, had Victoria to tell? That Lilac had not been in Seacastle at all on Thursday night or Friday or Saturday—yes, but Simon's information put Lilac here in her car at about five o'clock on Sunday, and Olive Stacey placed the time of Lilac's telephone call at about eight o'clock the same evening. More recent reports, and therefore more valuable than Victoria's own bewilderment.

Wait, thought Victoria stubbornly, wait just a little longer. . . .

". . . infuriating!" said Millicent, running the zipper of her bag back and forth in a two-inch line. She gave a final angry wrench; the zipper came free and she burrowed for the saccharine tablets. "There now, I must have lost at least an ounce getting at them. . . . I suppose you've been driven mad with phone calls, Victoria."

Shortly after that, Victoria left the house and got into her cab. Rain struck at her face, swung the skirts of her coat, followed her in a last wet flurry as she closed the door of the taxi. She gave the address of the Thall house, brushed raindrops from her purse, and looked for gloves that weren't there. The cab was just beginning to move, windshield wipers clicking. Victoria said, "Just a minute, driver," and was out of the cab and at Millicent's front door again. She had tossed her gloves on the couch when she first went in; mechanically, without thinking, she opened the door and heard Millicent say sharply into the telephone, "I told you not to call here again, it's dangerous. My husband will get——" She swung at the sound of the door.

"I'm sorry. My gloves," said Victoria, and picked them up and went out again under Millicent's motionless stare.

Millicent had lost no time in calling Mr. Fox back, she thought, as the cab crept along the narrow wet road fronting the bay. Was there a link between this telephone call and the knowledge concerning Freddy Spencer and his wife that had to be kept from Simon? There had been something else odd in Millicent's house, a tiny, fragmentary wrongness somewhere that had poked at Victoria's consciousness before it slid out of mind. . . .

She didn't have time to speculate. Because, not long after she returned to the Thall house, the chaos of official investigation began, and in the middle of it she was asked to identify the frightening thing they had found under a rotted pier in the harbor behind the hill.

CHAPTER 6

THE Halliday station wagon stood in the driveway when Victoria paid the cab driver and ran across the sodden lawn, head bent against the wet lash of rain. At the library window to the left of the front door, hands cupped against the streaming panes, Olive Stacey talked cajolingly to Shandy. "Down, boy. You'll get your breakfast in a few minutes. . . ."

She turned at Victoria's breathless apology, smiling under the brim of a dripping sou'wester. "I thought he'd be driving you mad by this time so I brought over some food. . . . Nonsense, I didn't mind at all." She looked down at her long oilskin coat. "We dress for these things in Seacastle. But you'd better get inside, you're drenched."

Olive's pointed face had a pinched gray look, and there were pockets of shadow under her restless brown eyes. In the kitchen, stirring milk into a bowl of dog food while the Saint Bernard nosed at the table edge, she said bluntly, "I'm afraid, Miss Devlin. I can't see Lilac letting Simon, letting us all, worry like this if she could possibly get to a phone. Simon won't believe anything could have happened to her, but—"

Victoria's heart contracted. It was the flat statement of her own slowly growing fear, but it was peculiarly shocking, as though a blurred and indistinguishable picture had suddenly leaped into crystal-sharp focus. She said nothing, because there was nothing to say, and after a moment Olive put the bowl of dog food on the floor and went to the sink to wash her hands. Rain beat against the windows in the pause that followed; mechanically, Victoria switched on the kitchen light and began to make coffee.

Olive turned from the sink, a paper towel in her hands. She said slowly, "I've been thinking. . . . Last Wednesday, when Lilac was found that way in her car. Suppose she hadn't taken those aspirins as she said, or—anything else. Suppose someone had given her a drug of some sort, someone she wanted to protect? She was very short with the police, you know. She didn't want to talk about it at all, said it was nothing to bother about. . . ."

It was the thing that had been lingering darkly in the back of Victoria's mind. She said, "But who? And why?"

"I don't know why. But Lilac would protect Millicent. Or," Olive's voice hardened, "Charles Storrow."

Charles Storrow, his gray eyes wide with worry, his young honest voice rough with it . . . "Or Simon," said Victoria coolly.

"Simon?" Amused incredulity; was there a flicker of something else besides? "I think," said Olive in her precise voice, "that we can leave Simon out of it. After all, he—"

The doorbell rang then. Victoria left Olive standing at the sink and opened the door on two hours of questions and answers and photographs and telephone calls.

There were six reporters, two state policemen, and a tall quiet-voiced man whose official identity she immediately forgot. At the very rear, his affable face resigned and a little mocking, came Sergeant Tansill.

One of the reporters said, "This the sister?" and a flash bulb went blindingly off in Victoria's face. Another voice said, "Nope. That's the Beautiful Blonde Childhood Friend of the missing heiress," and Victoria turned away from another stinging burst of light. The quiet man in gray touched her arm and said, indicating the library, "If you'll come in here with me, Miss Devlin, we can shut the door on those vultures."

The library was cold, filled with muted under-water dimness from the rain-cloaked windows. The man in gray sat down behind the desk and Victoria took the green leather armchair near the fireplace, conscious of the state trooper near the door, writing in a pad on his knee. There was no sign of Sergeant Tansill. In the tiny interval that passed while the man at the desk glanced at pencilled notes, Victoria had time to decide between the truth and the version she had already given. The logical conclusion was stark and final. If Lilac were still in hiding for some unguessed reason of her own, continued secrecy was essential. If something had happened to her here in Seacastle, then information about her clandestine trip to New York couldn't help the police in their search for William Fowler, could have no bearing on what must be another brutal and motiveless crime.

"Now, Miss Devlin—"

It began. They were the same questions that she had been asked earlier, but sharpened and embroidered and far more intent. How long had she known Lilac Thall? Was this purely a chance visit or had she reason to believe that Lilac was ill or in trouble? Had she any positive indication of when Lilac had last been in the house on Sunday? Was the dead woman, Alma Corey, the kind of nurse who would leave a patient alone lightly? Had Lilac's condition been such that it would have been dangerous to leave her? Was it conceivable that the invalid could have slipped out of the house unseen by Victoria and Nurse Corey on Sunday afternoon? Had she been in the shed since she arrived in Seacastle—had she seen the sickle?

The stony answers—truth, and the guarded skirting of the truth. She hadn't entered the shed at all. She had known Lilac for nine years, they had met at Miss Harvey's Academy in Boston. During the past year, Lilac had invited her repeatedly to visit her in Seacastle; she had by chance picked an unfortunate week-end. Nurse Corey had not allowed anyone to see Lilac, but Victoria had called to her from the doorway. . . .

"Isn't it odd, Miss Devlin, that there wasn't a doctor in attendance if Miss Thall was ill enough to require the services of a nurse?"

"But there was." Olive Stacey had slipped unobtrusively into the library; she stood with green tweed shoulders braced against the door. She said, "Dr. Misham had seen Lilac—Miss Thall—last week, at the start of her illness. He insisted that she get a complete rest immediately, and a nurse, if possible, to insure it."

Victoria gazed at the legs of the desk, trying to conceal her surprise. Lilac's plans had been really thorough then, but how ... ? The unfinished question in her own mind was answered by Olive's calm voice. "I'm afraid you won't be able to get in touch with Dr. Misham himself—I understand he's on a cruise at present—but he left instructions with his nurse. I imagine she'd be able to tell you more accurately just what Miss Thall's condition was."

Of course. Seacastle was a small town, and relationships were fairly public property. The policeman who found Lilac senseless in her car, realizing that he could hardly bring her back to her own empty house, had taken her to her fiancé's, and Dr. Misham had been called. Complete rest would have been the routine prescription, particularly if the patient had been vague and a little frightened and complained of a headache so severe that she had taken, several aspirin. ...

There were more questions. At the end of an hour Victoria's rigid composure cracked; she leaned forward and had said desperately, "What's the use of all this? It's that man from the sanitarium you ought to find, isn't it? He killed Nurse Corey, he—"

"We're doing everything we can to find William Fowler, I assure you, Miss Devlin. Meanwhile—"

Abruptly, Victoria understood. Lilac Thall might not be heiress to anything more than the house in Seacastle; she was nevertheless a member of an old and socially prominent Boston family. Furthermore, she was engaged to the son of another powerful Boston line—Simon Halliday, whose grandfather had been in the legislature, whose father had been a noted judge. There had to be reporters and photographs and officials and a dignified display of the law. ...

Was that Simon's voice in the hall? Victoria caught herself straining to listen, and was aware that the man at the desk was talking to her and rising. "We'd like you to stay in Seacastle until Miss Thall is found, Miss Devlin— you can arrange that, can't you?"

"Yes, of course." It was Simon, and someone else. Rufe?

There was a tap at the library door. Victoria turned her head expectantly as it opened, but it wasn't Simon. The other state policeman came in, followed by Sergeant Tansill. The trooper said, "I thought you'd want to see this right away, sir. Sergeant Tansill and I were taking a look along the shore near where the nurse was killed. We found this snagged on a branch underneath an old pier."

The object changed hands. It was still wet; it left a tiny trail of drops along the glass-topped desk as the tall man in gray held it out to Victoria. "Ever seen this before, Miss Devlin?"

She hadn't. It was a grayish pink square of sodden wool, torn at one corner, with a scattering of tarnished gold sequins near the jagged edge. Victoria knew what it was even before Olive looked and whitened and said, the words dropping like stones, "Oh . . . my . . . God. That's Lilac's," and put a shaking hand over her eyes.

Lilac dead. Lilac's lungs filled with water, her body washing lazily somewhere in the harbor . . . Victoria was aware of Simon's hand on her arm, the fingers biting into her flesh. "Don't, Victoria. It doesn't mean . . . they aren't sure—"

It's my fault, thought Victoria, unable to stop the tears running down her still face. If I hadn't agreed to the whole wild plan Nurse Corey would be alive, Lilac would be here. Oh why, why did I ever say I'd do it?

Rufe's hand was on her other arm, his voice saying with remembered gentleness, "Take it easy, kid. Wait till we can get somewhere—"

Victoria turned her head and saw with remote astonishment that his eyes were wet too. She choked and said, "Oh, God. Lilac," and a flash bulb flared in her eyes. It woke her, despising the mockery of grief she would see in tomorrow's newspapers, loathing the crisp voices of reporters in the hall. "That's the guy she's engaged to, on the left—hold it, please, Mr. Halliday. Swell. Now if you'll stand alone a minute . . ."

"Get out of here," said Simon quietly. "Get the hell out of here before—" He dropped Victoria's arm and stepped forward. Rufe said sharply, "Steady, Simon!"

"Yes. Don't," said Victoria unsteadily, and put her hand on Simon's sleeve as Rufe went forward to talk to the reporters. An abstract portion of her mind noted that an emergency had had a calming effect on Rufe's voice and hands and eyes; they could hear him saying reasonably, "Look, you've got all the pictures you need, haven't you? How about dropping it for a while and coming back later?"

The reporters left then. One of them darted back into

the living room and stripped from its frame a portrait of
Lilac looking gay and sardonic in a sweater and pearls. Simon made an abrupt movement of impotent fury and Rufe
said gently. "Let it go. They'd get hold of it somehow anyway."

Blessedly, the house was emptied of newspapermen
and police. They wandered into the living room, empty and
aimless, not meeting each other's eyes. Rufe said firmly,
"I'll make us all a drink," and disappeared in the direction
of the kitchen.

His absence created a gap; Rufe had been the one sta-
bilizing factor in the shock and horror that had followed
the discovery of Lilac's pink and gold kerchief. They all
began to talk at once, urgently saying nothing.

"It doesn't necessarily mean—"

"They won't know anything until . . ."

"Millicent," said Olive suddenly. "I don't think anyone's told Millicent—hadn't we better let her know before
the police do?"

They stared at each other. Simon said with an effort,
"I suppose we should," and Victoria looked at the rug and
said dully, "She ought to know. Even though there's nothing . . . certain. Shall I?"

Olive shook her head. "I'll phone."

Water ran and ice clicked distantly in the kitchen.
From the library came the smooth spin of the dial, and Ol-
ive's voice saying gently, "Millicent? This is Olive. I'm at
Lilac's. . . ."

Sight and sound ebbed away from Victoria. She
thought blankly and incredulously, I killed her. By coming
here, by letting Lilac go off on too dangerous an errand, I
sent her to her death. I should have known, I should have
remembered that her schemes were always too bold and
too daring. But I let her go, into the water—how long is it
before the sea casts them up? Oh, Lilac, Lilac—

Simon had crossed the room, had her cold hands in
his. He said in a low voice, "Stop it, Victoria. You
couldn't, none of us could have—"

But I could, cried Victoria soundlessly, I could! She
tried to free her hands and Simon held them, his own
warm and strong. She stopped trembling and went limp
and quiet, and Simon said, "That's better," and stepped
back abruptly when Rufe came in with drinks.

Millicent had taken the news very well, Olive said,

settling herself on the couch a few moments later. A state trooper had been over to question her earlier, she said, and she refused to accept the finding of the water-logged kerchief as proof that Lilac was . . . Even Olive's brisk tongue balked at the dreadfully final word. She said, "Millicent's quite right, of course. It needn't necessarily mean . . ." She left it there. "I asked them both to dinner tonight—there's no point in their sitting home and brooding. You'll come, of course, Victoria?"

Victoria nodded mechanically. Simon shot her a quick glance. "Better come with us now. This place may be overrun with reporters, and there's nothing you can do here. If there's any—news, we'll hear it at once."

Not news, thought Victoria coldly; confirmation. Lilac's body washed up somewhere in water-soaked cinnamon tweed, her throat bearing the vicious marks of a sickle. Lilac hadn't, as the others believed, been alarmed at Miss Corey's absence and gone searching for the nurse in the dark. But she had returned to Seacastle and had been mixed up, in some incomprehensible way, with the telephone message that had sent Nurse Corey on her fatal trip over the hill. And Lilac herself had been next. . . .

Victoria shook her head and thanked them. She'd come over later; meanwhile, the police might return to the house and someone ought to be there.

"I'll stay." Rufe was urgent. "Do you good to get out of here, Victoria. You'd better go on with Simon and Olive."

They left without her, finally. Victoria collected glasses and ash trays and washed them intently, keeping her hands occupied with brisk familiar things. With the kitchen shining behind her, she went upstairs to tidy the room she had left so hurriedly in response to Millicent Spencer's phone call.

The police had been thorough, she thought, standing at the closet door with her housecoat over her arm. While she had been answering questions in the library, they had been searching here: pushing clothes to one end of the rod, moving her hat box and a dusty one of Lilac's. . . . The top shelf stretched surprisingly far back into dimness but they had penetrated there too. Victoria could just see the edge of a cardboard carton marked with pale smudges where reaching fingers had disturbed the even coating of dust.

She had stood like this once before, on Sunday night

after dinner with Nurse Corey, when she had noticed that the door was slightly ajar, that a scarf had fallen to the floor and her hat box was at a disturbed angle. She had thought at the time that it had been the maid, Angie Harris, casting an inquisitive eye over her wardrobe. But at the back of her mind even then, and startlingly clear now, was Nurse Corey's voice saying casually, ". . . I was looking for some addresses in an old book in the bedroom I used to have."

Had the dead woman been searching for something else, here in Lilac's closet?

Victoria brought a footstool and lifted the carton down carefully. It held the usual collection of things too old to be of any use, too linked with associations to be thrown away. A pair of long, yellowed doeskin gloves were wound around a scattering of brittle fabric daisies, painstakingly removed from some forgotten hat. There were three or four snapshots—Millicent with a tennis racket, Lilac in a group, Mrs. Thall, looking stuffed, a laughing boy and girl whom Victoria didn't recognize.

The contents of the box seemed suddenly pitiable. These were the things Lilac had saved, these were the tangible shapes of the memories she hadn't wanted to lose. Victoria brushed hair away from her forehead, seeing a silver chain evening bag and a length of faded blue velvet through a blur.

It was under the velvet that she found the diaries, small thin volumes with a date written on the flyleaf of each in Lilac's round rambling hand: January, 1939, March, 1940 . . . The police had prowled through these too, the dusty covers were freshly thumbed. The diaries continued, with the exception of 1941, through 1944.

Victoria sat back on her heels, listening to the thin steady whipping of rain against glass, aware of a faint stir of excitement under blanketing numbness. Wasn't it odd that so methodical a chronicler should have skipped a whole year—and then returned to the same kind of volume, the same round hand? Or had something happened in 1941, something the police were more than cursorily interested in?

Victoria sent her mind back. 1941—Pearl Harbor and the first uniforms, upswept hair and their graduation from Miss Harvey's Academy. Lilac had been sick that spring, and her parents had packed her off with Nurse Corey for three weeks in Bermuda; she had returned with a magnificent rosy tan that sent suspicious numbers of students scurrying to the sun-lamp in the school infirmary. But it was too long ago for Victoria to remember anything else that might have mattered.

Unless—had there been something odd about Lilac's illness?

She stood up, stiff and chilled, and climbed on the footstool again and replaced the carton. It wasn't important. Lilac's death in the water had nothing to do with an eight-year-old diary; she and Victoria had planned it between them last Thursday night as surely as though they had oiled and loaded a gun.

Rain surged against the windows, drowning the blurred outline of the hill. A tiny clear trickle squeezed triumphantly under the sill; Victoria wiped it away without feeling the coldness on her fingers. If only she had refused any part in this tragic plan. If only . . .

Six o'clock. Victoria sat on a pale striped satin love seat in Grace Halliday's living room and said to an inquiring voice above her, "What? . . . Oh, I'm sorry. Martini, please."

She had arrived with Simon only a few minutes ago. Millicent and Freddy Spencer were already there, standing with Olive beside the fire. Victoria felt an unwilling admiration for Lilac's sister. She had deliberately avoided the dark colors the other women had instinctively chosen, and the periwinkle blue of her dress made her pretty face flushed, her eyes deeper than ever. There was a faint air of defiance in the way she lifted her glass to her lips, in her clear voice saying to Freddy, "May I have a cigarette, darling? If it really kills your appetite, as they say, I'll take it up as a habit. . . ."

There had been a peculiar little scene a few minutes ago when Grace Halliday, grave and slender in black, had come downstairs to greet them. "Millicent. My dear . . ." Sympathy, falling delicately short of condolence; the older woman had put out a hand to Millicent. And startlingly, so abruptly that it brought color up into Grace Halliday's face, Millicent had recoiled from the outstretched hand, saying crisply, "Don't be sorry for me, please, Mrs. Halliday. I don't believe it, you know."

The others had covered the awkwardness almost at

once; Rufe inquiring if Millicent would like a rye or a scotch old-fashioned, Olive moving forward to ask a question about dinner, Freddy Spencer, red with embarrassment, saying earnestly to no one, "Frightful shock, of course, but nothing conclusive, nothing conclusive at all. . . ."

At the love seat, Simon said, "Yours, I think." Victoria took the glass he handed her and went restlessly across to the deep window beside the fireplace. It was like a very chic and elegant wake, she thought, with firelight and superlative cocktails and murmuring, changing patterns of people delicately not mentioning the deceased. At her side Rufe said softly, "God, isn't this ghastly?"

His eyes swept the room broodingly. Victoria, not answering, followed his bleak inclusive glance at pale silvery green broadloom, cool gray walls, a brocaded wing chair, a couch with lines as simple and lovely as a seashell's. Lustres dripped and flashed on the white mantel; at the end of the room in a silver bowl, tulips lifted polished red heads that echoed softly out of a dim mirror. "I suppose it's better than going crazy separately," Rufe was saying, and then the telephone rang.

They had found Lilac—it flickered across every startled face. The phone rang again, and Grace Halliday said with forced calmness, "Olive dear, Esther is busy in the kitchen. Would you—"

"I'll get it," Rufe said, and caught the phone in mid-ring. After an unbearable moment of waiting silence, they could hear his voice in the hall: "Yes, she is. Just a minute, please."

Millicent gave a small whimpering cry, but Rufe was back in the doorway. "It's for you, Victoria."

Surprise and curiosity hidden quickly in lowered glances and casually lifted voices; Victoria put down her glass and went out into the hall. Her Aunt Ellen, in New York, was the only person who knew she was in Seacastle. She had seen the papers, probably, and was worried. An unanswered call to the Thall house would have increased her worry, spurred her to try the only other Seacastle connection she remembered from a long-ago summer. . . .

"Miss Devlin?" It was a man's voice, backgrounded by long-distance clicking and static. "This is Grayson's. On those cinnamon slipcovers we promised to have ready for you by Sunday night. I'm sorry, but there's been an unavoidable delay. We can have them for you at about eight o'clock tomorrow evening, if there'll be someone there to receive them."

Victoria made a sound.

"I hope," said the man remotely, "that you won't advertise this rapid service of ours, Miss Devlin, as we've made a very special exception in your case. Naturally, we're not set up at present to offer it to just everyone—"

"But . . ."

"—and of course we don't want to disappoint people, as we'd be forced to. But I'm sure you'll find everything satisfactory, and I hope you'll call on us again."

At the end of an eternity Victoria thanked the faraway voice and hung up. The edge of the telephone table bit into her palms as she gripped it to keep from swaying, the lighted hall around her vanished in a dipping dark-gold blur. She knew of no place called Grayson's. She had ordered no slipcovers.

It was, incredibly, a message from Lilac. Lilac was alive, and she was coming back to Seacastle.

CHAPTER 7

LILAC wasn't dead, she hadn't drowned in the icy black harbor. . . . Victoria felt light and boneless with relief as the weight of tragedy and her own guilt dissolved. Opposite her, the mirror with the whirling mahogany edges cleared again and she saw her face caught in the shining glass—cheeks filled with radiant pink, eyes as wide and brilliant as an excited child's. Over her navy blue shoulder was a reflected angle of the living room; the maid went through it with canapes on a tray, someone murmured, "Not for me, thanks."

There wasn't time now to exult in a safe sunny world after the boiling darkness of nightmare. Victoria used a powderpuff in an attempt to dim her own tell-tale glow. The message had been unmistakable—Lilac would be home tomorrow night at about eight, and Victoria was to be there at the house to meet her so that they could weave some sort of story between them. The warning had been just as definite. No one was to know.

It didn't occur to Victoria then to doubt the carefully couched message or the strange voice that had delivered it.

But how to face an evening that had suddenly become intolerable? Because they were convinced, all of them, just as she herself had been, that Lilac was dead—and Victoria, with a word, could bring her to life again: safe, unharmed, on her way back to Seacastle. And these, after all, were the people closest to Lilac—her sister and brother-in-law, her fiancé and his family.

But the telephone call settled it. Somewhere among them was the one Lilac feared.

Victoria went into the living room as casually as she could, said, "Aunt Ellen and her ultimatums," and picked up her unfinished cocktail. They had watched her briefly when she entered; at her careless words their attention fell away again to the one bleak reality that had brought them all together in Grace Halliday's cool stiff beautiful house.

It was Lilac to whom she owed her loyalty; she had to keep reminding herself of that, stonily, in order to hold to her unspoken promise of secrecy. . . . Over the rim of her glass, Victoria began to watch and listen with new awareness.

Was it Grace Halliday whom Lilac feared, slender and erect on the couch, her charming face withdrawn and troubled? Olive, who a moment later looked up at a murmured word from Grace, glanced at her watch and slipped quietly out of the room? Millicent Spencer, Lilac's plump, pretty sister who had been so unaccountably shaken by the telephone call from Mr. Fox that morning and who had since regained a good deal of her pink placidity? Or affable Freddy, who would hum his small nonchalant hum in the face of an earthquake?

Rufe had risen and gone into the small L of the living room; he listened to the chiming clock for a moment and then turned on the radio. Victoria watched his narrow gentle face as he waited with a guarded eye on the group at the other end of the room. A news announcer's voice, almost inaudible, said, ". . . were injured in the explosion. A three-state search continues tonight for William Fowler, escaped inmate of Bellemarsh Sanitarium, who is believed responsible for the killing of Louise Brainard, Elizabeth Cossett, and Nurse Alma Corey of Boston. Police are also seeking the whereabouts of—"

Simon had come up, his face still and expressionless. Rufe snapped off the dial and Simon turned it on again, grimly. The radio resumed impersonally, "—although clothing recovered in Seacastle Harbor indicates that—" This time it was Simon's hand that went out in a flashing movement that cut the voice into silence. Victoria, still watching, knew that she had intended all along to tell Simon that Lilac was alive.

It was worse at dinner. Millicent talked brightly of calories and energy units and a new diet based largely on eggplant, and in the middle of it burst into tears and fled from the room. For a moment, shocked into helplessness, they all sat frozen in a pattern of napkins and silver and barely-touched food. Then Freddy was out of his chair and going nimbly into the living room, and Victoria had cried wrenchingly, "Oh, but—"

Faces woke and turned towards her; Victoria felt suddenly trapped under their eyes. Was there too much expectancy there, too tight an air of waiting? In the living room, Millicent had stopped crying, Freddy's low voice emerged in a soothing blur. Victoria heard herself saying weakly, "But there's nothing. . . . Nobody knows yet—"

I can't do this, she thought, it's more than anyone has a right to ask. Around her, after a hushed consultation, the others had resumed a pretense of dining. Simon alone hadn't moved, he sat staring at flowers in the center of the table as though his sanity were contained in tulips and ferns, his face so cold that it might have worn a thin invisible shell of ice.

Millicent came back presently and gave them all a damp brave smile. "I'm sorry I went off like that. It won't help, will it? And after all, as Freddy says, the police haven't given up yet, so why should we?"

Saved, thought Victoria, folding her napkin into intricate headwaiter shapes. She had come perilously close to following Millicent into the living room to tell her that Lilac was alive and would return tomorrow night—and to repose a secret in Lilac's sister was the height of futility.

She found the opportunity she had been waiting for when they went back into the living room for coffee. Going over to the recessed window beside the fireplace, she said quietly, "Simon, drive me home, will you? There's something I want to tell you."

"Certainly," said Simon politely and without interest, and Victoria moved away again to join the others.

Nearly an hour later, at the door, Grace Halliday was curiously reluctant to let Simon go. Her brows went up over the fine dark eyes as Simon belted his raincoat. "Going out, dear? Oh—how stupid of me, I thought the Spencers were dropping Miss Devlin off on their way."

"Glad to," said Freddy with an inquiring look at Victoria.

"And I know Miss Devlin will excuse you, under the circumstances." Simon's aunt slanted her dark head a little, smiling apologetically at Victoria. Her expression said confidingly that Simon was under too great a strain to be ferrying dinner guests hither and yon, and Victoria, annoyed, felt herself flushing. She said lightly, "It *is* a nuisance. Suppose I—"

"Nonsense, it's a pleasure," said Simon curtly, and then they were out in blowing, splashing darkness. Victoria waited until they had moved into the road behind the red tail-light of the Spencer's car before she said, "Simon, Lilac's alive. She's coming back tomorrow. That phone call I had before dinner was a message from her—"

That was as far as she got. The car gave a violent lurch, Simon slowed it to a saner crawl, said, "Oh my God. Are you sure?" and began to ask questions. Had she recognized the man's voice? If Lilac was all right why hadn't she come to the phone herself? Widely publicized disappearances like this one always brought up a brimming netful of cranks—how could they be sure that this wasn't a ruse of some sort, someone's perverted practical joke?

Victoria kept back the impatient answers that tumbled to her lips. The cloaked reference to Lilac's cinnamon tweeds, the suit she had been wearing last; the careful mention of Sunday night as the promised delivery date for the "slipcovers"—but if Simon knew that he would know everything, and the whole painstaking web of plans and subterfuge would unravel, leaving Lilac exposed.

Simon swung the car into the Thall driveway. The headlights flared briefly into the darkness, turning the wet lawn and huddled shrubs into a dripping gilt frieze against the blackness beyond. Simon looked intently at Victoria in the dim glow from the dashboard and said abruptly, "Was I supposed to be told about this? Was that in the message, too?"

"Of course." She had been braced for that and she answered it too quickly and with more emphasis than it deserved. Simon knew she was lying: the alert pose of his head and the flat silence that stretched between them said so plainly. Victoria covered embarrassment and a stab of pity with small crisp movements of departure, picking up her gloves and bag, twisting the door handle, saying a little stiffly, "Thank you for bringing me home." But Simon was out of the car too. "I'd better take Shandy for a run. You couldn't manage him—he'd be in the next county in nothing flat."

In the living room she moved aimlessly about, lighting lamps and emptying ashtrays, looking nervously at the clock and remembering Grace Halliday's unconcealed reluctance to have Simon drive her home. Why? Was it because, with Lilac presumably out of the way, Simon's aunt wanted no more alliances, however slight? But that was ridiculous, she thought, listening to Simon's distant shout, because that would mean that there was an advantage to Grace in Simon's not marrying after all—and what advantage could there possibly be? Not financial, because the money that allowed Grace to maintain a leisured existence in a beautiful home had been left to her by her husband, Elliot Halliday. Rufe had said as much when Victoria had admired a Sargent in the dining room earlier that evening. "Nice, isn't it? Part of Uncle Elliot's estate—he had a small collection but a very good one, I believe. Happily for Aunt Grace and the lawyers, that seems to have been his only extravagance."

Victoria caught herself up with a feeling of distaste. It had gotten to be second nature in the past few days, this prying scrutiny of faces and voices and the most innocent of actions. It was all but over now. If Lilac arrived on time tomorrow night she could get on a plane and be back in her own apartment before midnight. . . .

Simon was back. Shandy shook himself vigorously and padded to the living room doorway to wave his tail amiably at Victoria. "He's getting fond of you," Simon said. "That amounts to a wild demonstration." He moved toward the door and turned with a hand on the knob. "You'll be all right here tonight?"

"Of course. I'll lock everything and entice your friend upstairs with a biscuit. And Simon—you'll be awfully careful, won't you, about not letting anyone find out about Lilac? It's horribly cruel, I know, but—"

"I suppose there's a reason. As long as she's all right—" Simon opened the door. "Thanks for telling me about it, Victoria," he said quietly, and closed it behind him.

With the Saint Bernard at her heels, Victoria went carefully over the first floor, checking doors and windows.

Locking up was a terrifying process, she thought; each clicking mechanism, every sliding bolt underscored the nervousness you might have been able to ignore otherwise. At every door was the spurring sense of hurry to get on to the next, because that might be the very one, and while you were busy at this window the one behind you might be slipping soundlessly up to let in the night and the hostile hands. There was panic just beneath the surface in this ritual of securing the house against hours of darkness. . . .

The sound of the phone sent a shock of weakness through her. It was Charles Storrow, his voice impatient and eager. He had tried to reach her earlier, he said; had she happened to notice anywhere around the house Lilac's engagement book?

"One of those small things women carry in bags," said Charles. "Green, I'm pretty sure."

Victoria hadn't seen it, hadn't known Lilac ever used one. She said, "Is it important?" and his voice came back. "It is to me. Lilac had an appointment on the afternoon she was drugged. Mrs. Spencer just remembered that she said something about it—and if somebody didn't want her to go wherever she was going . . ."

Lilac drugged so that she wouldn't turn up at a certain place at a specified time—it was frighteningly logical. None of the others had mentioned Lilac's having had an appointment that day, but perhaps only Millicent had known. Millicent, whose sweetness had always been founded on an acid base.

"In her purse?" Charles Storrow was asking hopefully. "I suppose the police took that with them, though . . ."

But they hadn't, Victoria thought moments later, hanging up after promising to look for the little engagement book. Lilac's brown calf purse had been missing before the police had come to the house, because she had realized on Monday afternoon, when Rufe and Simon and Grace Halliday and Freddy Spencer had all joined in the search for a note from Lilac, that the handbag was mysteriously not there.

The Saint Bernard eyed her mournfully from the doorway. Victoria turned out the lights and brought a dog biscuit and a bowl of milk to the second floor landing, and could hear the comforting rattle of Shandy's collar as she undressed with bath water running. In bed, the disturbing thought that she had deliberately not faced all evening came to stare at her in the darkness.

If the long-distance call and its implications were genuine, Lilac had been delayed on her errand. It was inconceivable that she should have returned secretly to Seacastle on Sunday afternoon, for the purpose of being seen by Simon and Charles Storrow, and then have gone as secretly back to New York.

No. Someone else, who knew her mannerisms and her way of driving, had taken her car and worn her kerchief and made a telephone call to convey the impression that she was in Seacastle.

Someone close to Lilac.

Olive arrived the next morning while Victoria and Shandy were breakfasting in the kitchen. She didn't stay long. She had brought the morning newspapers; there might be people telephoning and she thought Victoria ought to be prepared. "You made page eight yourself," she said with a twisted smile, and then, "Yes, I'd love a cup of coffee, if you have lots."

She apparently did not only the ordering and telephoning and errand-running for the Hallidays but also the worrying, Victoria thought, looking at her across the table. Her pointed face was tallowy with strain, and the burgundy wool of her smartly-cut suit drained all the color from her eyes and hair. Her only flicker of animation came from the fact that Simon had gone in to the office that morning.

"Thank God for *that*," Olive said bluntly, stirring her coffee. "He's like a madman, of course, and there's nothing he can really accomplish by staying out here and haunting the police. He's been worried about business, too—there's some sort of crisis pending and the other partners have been threatening a meeting for weeks. I don't know what it's all about, but if it can only take his mind off—off Lilac for a few hours . . ."

Victoria glanced down at her own cup. Better get used to this, she thought, it's going to go on all day. With a sudden spurt of courage she asked Simon's cousin whether she knew if Lilac had had an appointment on the afternoon of the day she was drugged.

Olive had risen and was pulling on her gloves. Gazing down at Victoria, mechanically smoothing suède over her fingers, she said, "Appointment? That was last Wednesday, wasn't it? It seems so long ago. . . . I suppose she could have had an appointment later on, after the hairdresser, although I don't remember her saying anything about it. Does it make any difference—now?"

"I suppose not." Over Olive's shoulder, through the kitchen window, Victoria watched a car nosing into the driveway. Moments later a door slammed, and Sergeant Tansill's head and shoulders went bobbing up the path.

Olive had seen him too. She said, grimacing, "Oh, Lord. You've been taking the brunt of this, Victoria—do you want me to stay? I can say you're not feeling well, if you like."

The doorbell rang. Victoria swallowed her guilt, said, "Thanks, but it's all right," and went into the hall to say good-bye to Olive and greet Sergeant Tansill. Cautiously, because here was where she had to be most guarded of all.

"Good-morning, Sergeant. I suppose there isn't any news yet?"

"Not yet, Miss Devlin. Chesterton"—that must be the tall man in gray who had questioned her in the library yesterday—"and the powers that be have gone into a huddle about dragging the harbor. They can drag it," said Sergeant Tansill brusquely, "till hell freezes over. A harbor this size, with currents like these—you'd play hide and seek with a body for days. Now that young lawyer two years ago that was lost off his sailboat . . ." He glanced at Victoria, reddened a little, and said, "But that isn't what I came to ask you about, Miss Devlin."

"Yes, Sergeant?" They were in the living room, the sergeant seated distrustfully on the edge of the yellow corduroy chair, Victoria on the couch.

"Are you sure Nurse Corey had a key to the house?"

"Yes, positive."

"We didn't find it," the sergeant said slowly. "Not in her purse or her clothes or on the ground around where she was killed. Seems odd that he'd take that, and nothing else."

'He'—William Fowler, the frightful phantom she had driven to the back of her mind because Lilac was alive after all. For a moment his shadow hovered closer, prowling in darkness, amused at her futile attempts to lock the house against danger. . . .

"Better have the lock changed," Sergeant Tansill was saying flatly. "I'll send a man up today."

Victoria followed him out into the hall. On a little table beneath the mirror were the newspapers Olive had brought. A headline in the top edition caught her eye: "Continue Search for Missing Girl." Two sub-heads said, "Lilac Thall may be Fourth Victim of Seacastle Sickle Killer; Brunette Socialite was Engaged to Wed."

It was probably, thought Victoria, one of the more subdued reports. She said, "There won't be any need to give Lilac's diary to the papers, will there, Sergeant? It was just a schoolgirl's thing, after all, and it can't have any bearing on what's happened. But you know what they'd do with it. . . ."

Sergeant Tansill had picked up his overcoat. He put it down on the chair again and turned a suspiciously amiable face to Victoria. "Diary? Now, how do you like that? Suppose you tell me what diary you're talking about, Miss Devlin?"

CHAPTER 8

"OH, BUT didn't you—?" Victoria struggled with bewilderment.

Sergeant Tansill didn't answer directly. He went past her into the library, picked up the phone, and dialled. After a few brief questions he said, "Thanks, I didn't think so," and hung up. "Now, Miss Devlin, if you'd be good enough to show me where you made this—discovery?"

Victoria flushed at the coolness of his voice and led the way silently upstairs to the bedroom closet. Sergeant Tansill lifted the box down gingerly, burrowed for the diaries and stared in bitter speechlessness at the dusty, fingerprinted covers. "You're all over them now," he said accusingly. "Still, we'll have a try. Why didn't you tell us about this before, Miss Devlin—"

"Because I only found them yesterday afternoon, after the house had been brimming with state police and reporters. Naturally I presumed that you, or one of the police, had taken the missing one."

"You knew they were here, though?"

"No. I just happened to look through the box. . . ." The warmth was back in her cheeks. Sergeant Tansill stared at her searchingly, shrugged and rose, the diaries in his hands. "I'll take these along. If someone's been in the house going through Miss Thall's personal things it puts a slightly different light on the matter. I suppose it's possible, of course, that Miss Thall herself . . ." he gazed at the slender volumes, his eyes thoughtful, and then departed.

The rain had stopped in the night; the morning was bleak and windy, washed to a colorless gray. After Sergeant Tansill left, Victoria got her coat and went restlessly out the kitchen door, through the wind-tattered garden and up the hill behind the house. Long grass brushed coldly against her legs as she stood on the hill and looked down with detached horror at the place where Nurse Corey had been murdered.

It was desolate, even by daylight. To her right, a tall gray beanpole fence sloped unevenly down to the shore; to her left the Thall property was bounded by a low stone wall. Just beyond the wall was the narrow grass-grown dead end lane that had once led to the rotted pier under which Lilac's kerchief had been found. And on this side of the wall, inside that shivering coppice of beeches, the nurse's stained and twisted body had lain, perhaps thirty feet up the slope from the lacy white hem of the harbor.

The wind whipped at Victoria's soft pale hair. She wasn't aware of it. She was remembering all at once that it had been Millicent's telephone call that had taken her out of the house yesterday morning, and that that was the only interval, with the exception of the undetermined segment of time before she had returned with Simon on Sunday evening, when the house had been empty.

Millicent hadn't really needed her that morning. She had been well enough to leave her bed immediately after Victoria left and telephone the unknown Mr. Fox. Had her real purpose been to bring Victoria out on a pretext, so that Freddy could enter the house and remove Lilac's diary for the year 1941? But she had locked the house behind her, and there had been no broken windowpanes, no forced locks.

William Fowler had Nurse Corey's key. Or—the thought that brushed Victoria's mind was so frightful that she thrust it almost physically away, finding a package of cigarettes in her pocket and lighting one, walking briskly along the crest of the hill.

But the chill had penetrated. Millicent had called Freddy at the Halliday home yesterday morning to ask him to drive Victoria over. So that anyone there would have known that Lilac's house was going to be empty.

Victoria looked at the harbor, at the rhythmic march of small waves that darkened and silvered and spun themselves into foam. Lilac was coming back, and that was all that really mattered now.

Meanwhile, there was the day to be gotten through somehow.

The newspapers. There was a two-column cut of Lilac in sweater and pearls, the one they had snatched from its frame yesterday. There was one of Victoria, her white face averted and featureless, with, incredibly, Simon's hand on her shoulder and a fraction of Rufe at one edge. "Fiancé of missing girl comforts friend," said the caption sardonically.

There was an editorial on the laxness of the sanitarium authorities in permitting William Fowler to escape, and a lengthy defensive statement by the superintendent of Bellemarsh. Simon stared furiously out of a tabloid's spot-scene page. One enterprising reporter had drawn a map of the Thall grounds, labeled, "Scene of Murder and Disappearance."

Vagrants and other suspicious characters were being held for questioning in three states. Would the Fowler-Thall case turn out to be an indictment of the entire Massachusetts penological system? Editorial opinion hinted darkly that it would.

Victoria threw the papers away, and wondered what tomorrow's editions would say when Lilac came ghosting back from the deep. It was eleven o'clock. In nine hours more ... Partly from a vague desire to reassure Millicent and partly from curiosity over the appointment she had mentioned to Charles Storrow, Victoria called the Spencer house.

Millicent said, "Victoria! I was just going to call you," and then, "Have you seen the papers?"

"Yes. Olive brought them."

"They have no right to assume like that that Lilac is—is dead. But I suppose," said Millicent slowly, "that she is. Freddy thinks so, and he says it will—you know, hurt less if I face it. He says I mustn't make myself ill over the waiting until they—find her."

Victoria felt a little as though she were bearing water to a dying man in the desert who had turned out not to be thirsty at all. She said cautiously, "Oh, I wouldn't give up all hope yet, Millicent."

"We were very close," said Millicent's mournful voice. "You've no idea, Victoria, what it's like to lose a sister. No matter what Lilac ever did, or the little differences we've had, she was still my sister. And to think of the newspapers and all those vulgar reporters . . ."

She's enjoying it, thought Victoria, aghast. She's over the hurdle of shock, and somehow Freddy has made her see herself as brave and gallant in the face of tragedy. . . . Good Lord.

". . . of me, in *curlers*," Millicent was saying broodingly, "and I must say I don't think that was called for, under the circumstances."

Victoria cut her off, then, to ask about the appointment Lilac had mentioned on the day she was drugged, the day they had all lunched together at the Harbor Inn with Charles Storrow and the Hallidays.

"Oh—that. Charles was asking me last night, and I hadn't remembered before. Lilac did say something about an engagement later on."

"Do you remember what she said, Millicent?"

"No-o-o, not exactly. I'd been away fixing my face—it was after lunch—and when I got back to the table Freddy was asking Lilac if she wouldn't drop by at our house before dinner to have a cocktail and pick up some books she'd lent him. And she said—I can't remember what words she used—that she had to meet someone, and it was a date she'd been looking forward to and she couldn't break it. I can ask Freddy when he gets home tonight if you want—but what difference does it make now?"

"None, I suppose," said Victoria, and thanked her and hung up.

"Appointment?" echoed Grace Halliday at the other end of the line. "I don't think I—that was on Wednesday, wasn't it? Lilac went to her hairdresser's, of course. Could that be it?"

"I was thinking of later on, after that," Victoria said.

"Later on . . . I've a wretched memory," said Simon's aunt apologetically, "but I don't recall her having mentioned it. Were you thinking it had something to do with what happened to Lilac later on in her car, Miss Devlin?"

There was a hint of incredulity in her voice; the delicately arched brows would be raised, Victoria thought, and the upper lip lifted a little in a childishly inquiring curve. "I suppose it's possible," the warm voice went on, "but it does sound rather like one of Mr. Storrow's ten-reel notions."

Why were they all so anxious to discredit Charles Storrow, with careless pity or gentle contempt? Victoria looked down at the library desk and said coolly, "As a matter of fact, it was Mr. Storrow who mentioned it. But it was Millicent who spoke of it in the first place."

"Oh?" Grace Halliday's voice showed nothing more than polite disinterest. "Millicent would know, of course. But as for Mr. Storrow—I haven't met him more than once or twice, but I think you'll find he's a little on the melodramatic side, Miss Devlin."

Melodramatic—when as far as the rest of them knew Lilac had been killed and her body tossed into the harbor? Victoria was about to conclude the conversation when Grace asked pleasantly, "By the way, Miss Devlin, is it the police who are interested in this appointment Lilac may have had?"

... Or are you meddling on your own? Victoria finished it for her mentally, said, "No, not at the moment," and thanked her and put the receiver down.

It was odd, she thought, that the matter of the unexplained drugging had been allowed by the police to languish as long as it had. Or did they accept Lilac's thin explanation of too many aspirin, taken for a headache? In any case it had remained for Charles Storrow, of all the people who had been at the luncheon that day, to raise the question of the unkept appointment.

And that, of course, was the pivot of the whole thing—the reason why Lilac had come to Victoria's New York apartment in panic, the indirect cause of Nurse Corey's being brought to Seacastle and subsequently murdered.

Whom had Lilac been going to meet? And was that why her brown calf handbag had been removed from the house—because she had written a name and an hour in her little appointment book? Victoria moved to the window and looked out at the wet blot of lawn and the shining dark rhododendrons. Behind her, the grandfather clock began to strike noon. In a little more than eight hours, Lilac would walk through the door.

At close to one o'clock a policeman came and took Victoria's fingerprints. The familiar process that she had read about numberless times in books and newspapers was somehow bewildering; from now on the touch of her hand would be, officially, as concrete an identity as her own bones and body and speaking presence. When the policeman had gone she took a handkerchief from her bag, scrubbed her blurry fingertips and put the scrap of white linen away again. Halfway across the zipper balked; she tugged mechanically, freed a tiny edge of the handkerchief and eased the zipper closed in a silken run that was sharply, shockingly familiar.

It took her a moment to synchronize sight and sound into memory. The other bag with the stubborn zipper had been black calf, not suède, and it had been Millicent Spencer, propped against piled pillows in her bedroom, who pulled annoyedly at it. And the teeth on the zipper of Millicent's bag had been caught on a tiny soft shred of pale pink wool.

CHAPTER 9

MILLICENT at the wheel of the blue convertible, with Lilac's pink and gold kerchief over her dark hair, Millicent sounding the horn outside Charles Storrow's house while she extended a gloved hand with a cigarette in Lilac's nonchalant wave—Victoria felt curiously sick in the face, of what could only be wayward and uncontrollable malice.

Because how else could the kerchief have gotten into Millicent's handbag? And it had been there, the minute shred of pink shrieked its presence. Millicent hadn't noticed it because she had always been near-sighted; her blue eyes had that tell-tale appealing softness. She had thought the kerchief was safely disposed of, hadn't counted on the fragile fabric tearing when it was removed from her bag.

Victoria sat upright. Yesterday morning, when she had stood at the window of her bedroom staring out into the rain, she had put down as a part of the Seacastle landscape the oilskinned figure slipping hurriedly along the lane that skirted the Thall property and ran down to the harbor. Now she was almost certain that that was how the kerchief had found its way under the rotted remnant of the pier.

It was incomprehensible, but it fitted. It would explain, for instance, Millicent's conviction that Lilac wasn't dead, and her outburst at dinner the evening before when she had fled from the Hallidays' table in hysterical tears.

Remorse? Fear of detection? Or alarm because the ruse with the kerchief had carried matters much farther than she had intended?

Victoria pushed conjecture severely away. Lilac wasn't dead, and she must surely have prepared some sort of explanation for the police. Aside from a brief seething of publicity, she could resume her life in Seacastle as though nothing had happened; she would put the tragedy of Nurse Corey's death behind her in the flurry and excitement of her wedding to Simon.

Her wedding to Simon ... Victoria stared blankly at the halves of a cigarette that had snapped in her hands. She thought, clinging to a straw of comfort, You won't be here to see it. You won't have to watch them go away together—and realized, appalled, that the very idea was intolerable. There had been no warning growth, no tentative feeling to cut crisply and decisively at the root. Last night she had been merely sorry for Simon, aware of his lonely stubborn anguish, furious at Lilac for allowing it to go on. Now, at this moment, she knew only that she loved him, that it had had no beginning, that it could have no future.

It was a humiliatingly classic situation: the happy couple, the unwanted third. Whoever says it's best to face these things, thought Victoria remotely, is mad. The thing to do is get lunch, wash the dishes, hide from this feeling until it goes away.

She sliced tomatoes and cut her thumb, and put the gauze scrupulously away in the refrigerator.

It was certainly time to leave Seacastle.

She had a life of her own in New York. Her apartment, her friends, the job she had been lazily looking for. Better not scrutinize it too closely now—the world of inspired clothes and witty conversation, of cocktails with people she didn't care about and late evenings with more people she wished would go home; of lunches with other successful young career women and the job she would ultimately take on a fashion magazine, writing forecasts on the trend of a sleeve, the swerve of a silhouette, the devastating effect of Renoir Red.

I lived it before, thought Victoria in a kind of panic. I'll live it again, I'll forget all this. . . .

It was three o'clock, and then four and finally five. The police had come, and Victoria had repeated her account of events on Sunday evening. It took all the will power she possessed to face Chesterton, the tall man in gray who had questioned her earlier, and to watch Sergeant Tansill and a state policeman, accompanied by two reporters, go down the lane that led to the harbor. Lilac safe and unharmed, hundreds of miles away, while official machinery ground busily on . . .

Only a few hours more, she thought, bracing herself; then the truth, or whatever version of it Lilac chose to give—at the end of the brief recital she caught up her courage.

"Were there other fingerprints on the diaries, Mr. Chesterton? And was there anything important in the diaries themselves?"

Chesterton paused, hat in hand. "No prints worth anything but yours, Miss Devlin. As for the contents—" he shrugged. "I'm not familiar with young girls' diaries, but I'd say these were pretty much what you'd expect. Except that from 1942 Miss Thall seems to have been keeping something from herself, almost as though she were afraid the diaries might be read by someone else and there was something she didn't want to put down in black and white. Almost . . ." He broke off as the phone rang. "I believe that's the call I've been waiting for."

Victoria froze as he lifted the receiver, said, "Just a minute, please," and extended the phone. He didn't leave. He went as far as the doorway and took an envelope from his pocket and gazed at it absently as Victoria moved around the desk and picked up the receiver and said stonily, "Yes?"

It was Simon. His voice sang along her nerves and sent a rush of heat to her face. Victoria bent her head and thought despairingly, I'm behaving like a fool. I'll have to do better than this tonight. . . .

"I'm about to leave the office," Simon was saying rapidly. "I have to take a client out for a drink and I'm not sure when I can get rid of him. I'll come over tonight at a little before nine, shall I? Before you let the others know."

Chesterton was watching from the doorway. "All right," Victoria said stiffly.

"Victoria—is anything wrong? You heaven't heard anything from—?"

"Yes, the police are here," said Victoria with an effort at casualness.

"Sorry. You sounded odd, and I— Blast," Simon said abruptly. "See you tonight," and hung up.

In the door of the library, Chesterton replaced the envelope in his pocket. He said pleasantly, "By the way, did Sergeant Tansill tell you about Miss Thall's car? The steering wheel and gear shift and door handles were wiped clean—there were just some prints of yours on the fenders. Good-bye for now, Miss Devlin."

It was dark at a quarter of six, the wind was rising, sending a lonely echo about the corners of the house. Victoria drew the curtains across the mirroring black windows and went upstairs to pack. Fortunately for Lilac's plans there was no policeman about tonight, Sergeant Tansill had explained that the patrol in the town had been reinforced and he hadn't a man to spare. Victoria, controlling her relief, had replied that she wasn't nervous and there was always the phone. She dressed carefully, drawing out the time; the navy gabardine suit over a white blouse with snowy fluting that flared below her wrists and stood up softly about her throat, navy calf pumps with tall slender heels. She had laid out her hat and her gloves and was stowing bath powder and toothpaste in the suitcase on the bed when the doorbell rang, startlingly loud against the stillness of the house.

No one must know ahead of time that she was leaving. After a second of indecision, Victoria took off her suit jacket, closed the door of her room behind her and ran down the stairs.

It was Rufe Halliday. It seemed to Victoria, over-alert with the tension of waiting, that his glance around the hall and into the living room beyond it was quick and searching. He said, "I was driving past and thought I'd stop by and see if you were all right here. Have the police been around much?"

Victoria shook her head. "Just Mr. Chesterton—he's from the District Attorney's office, isn't he? And the local police, but they didn't come in."

Rufe nodded absently and sent his probing gaze around the living room again as he leaned against the mantel and said slowly, "Aunt Grace said you were asking about an appointment Lilac had that day last week."

It was a flat quiet statement with only a mild tone of interest; there was no reason at all for the warning, quickening pace of Victoria's heartbeats. "Yes, I was." She took a cigarette from the silver box beside her, and very suddenly Rufe was towering above the couch.

But he was only holding a match. Victoria leaned forward a little to light her cigarette, ashamed of her absurd panic just because Rufe had covered the distance between them so rapidly and so noiselessly. Still standing there, looking down at her with the wide-set troubled eyes that were like Simon's, Rufe dropped the burnt match into an ashtray and said, "I'd let it go, Victoria. It can't matter now—there's not much use in avoiding the fact any longer that if Lilac were alive they'd have found her by this time. And what's the use of stirring up more police questions? If what Lilac said about the aspirin wasn't true, she'd have known immediately that someone had given her a drug of some kind—which is preposterous—and she'd have told the police herself then and there."

Not if it would have meant exposing someone Lilac wanted to protect.

Not if—the thought was new and complex—Lilac herself had some reason to fear the police. Victoria lifted her eyes to meet Rufe's and said lightly, "I suppose you're right. But *did* you hear her mention an engagement later on?"

"No." Rufe turned abruptly away and took his hat from the arm of the yellow wing chair. "I gather this is Storrow's idea. If he asks you again I'd advise him to drop it too—he's not a very reliable witness as far as Lilac is concerned, you know. The poor guy was in love with her for years, and I suppose this is his way of tiding himself over the shock."

There it was again, the impatient brushing away of Charles Storrow as though he were a bad and insistent child. Victoria went with Rufe to the door. Shandy, arising from his favorite niche under the dining room table and knocking over a chair in the process, emerged to nose eagerly at the crack of darkness. Rufe bent and put a restraining hand on his collar. "Want me to take him out for you before I go?"

Victoria hesitated. Lilac was undoubtedly not nervous at night in her own home—but it would look odd if she dispatched Shandy to his owners ahead of time. She said, "No thanks, Rufe—I think I can manage him," and Rufe nodded and left.

Lilac's argued appointment on the day she was

drugged had certainly come very much to the fore, Victoria thought, mounting the stairs again. It was if they had all realized suddenly the latent danger in a situation that had been passed over before as upsetting but of no real importance.

It was nearly seven when she finished packing, and there was only a little more than an hour to wait. Victoria brought down her suitcase and hat and gloves, fed Shandy and went into the living room to read the remaining interval away.

This was the nerve-wracking time, when your mind refused to be diverted, when the clock was afflicted with creeping paralysis. This was when your consciousness dragged up a sombre parade of Things that Might Have Happened.

Lilac missing a train by seconds. A plane flight cancelled, although the night was clear and wind-scoured. This won't help, thought Victoria savagely, and turned a page and found herself staring at an illustration—Figure 7—of early Brussels lace.

At seven-thirty Freddy Spencer arrived.

Victoria let him in with a feeling of mingled rage and helplessness. And Freddy looked at her innocently and said, "Millie told me you called about some appointment Lilac was supposed to have had on Wednesday, so I drove right over after dinner."

"Oh—yes, I wondered if Lilac said where she was going."

Freddy had wandered into the living room; he sat down plumply on the end of the couch and shook his sandy head perplexedly. "Millie must have been mistaken. Lilac didn't say anything about an appointment—to me, anyway."

He's lying, thought Victoria, forgetting momentarily the clock and the approach of the danger period. Charles Storrow caught Millicent off guard and so did I, and she blurted out what she had heard Lilac say and now Freddy is retracting—why?

"I can't imagine," Freddy was saying thoughtfully, "what Millie could have heard that made her think Lilac was referring to an appointment, unless ..." Watching Freddy's face clear, Victoria had to concede that the look of enlightenment might have been genuine.

"What Lilac said," he remembered with an air of relief, "was that she always looked forward to getting home after a session with the hairdresser. That's it, that's why she begged off coming over for a cocktail."

"Oh." There wasn't much else to say, in spite of the fact that she didn't believe him. Freddy gave her the gay unclouded smile of a child waiting for a reward, and glanced across at the windows. "Cold night out," he said serenely.

Was he lingering deliberately? The time was going with frightening speed now that a visitor seemed to have taken root on the couch. At ten minutes of eight Victoria said shamelessly, "Millicent won't worry about your being gone so long, will she?" and maneuvered him as far as the hall. But even there Freddy halted, turning his hat brim in his hands, humming distractedly at it and breaking off to say tentatively, "Er—say, about that appointment business, Miss Devlin. Millie misunderstood, of course, but I think the less said about it the better. No use bringing her mind back to it, you know, harrowing her feelings and all that."

He was anxious, almost wheedling. Victoria promised him with wry truth that she wouldn't mention the matter again, and let out a breath of relief when the sound of his car died. It was over, the long and frightful waiting after accumulated days of uncertainty and dread. She had done what the message asked her to do, and the way was clear. She went into the living room and put A History of Lace back in the bookcase and lighted a cigarette. In the library, the grandfather clock clicked, whirred, and began to chime the hour.

At ten after eight Victoria said to herself, Naturally she wouldn't turn up on the dot like a genie out of a bottle.

At a quarter after Shandy growled in his throat and barked sharply. Victoria realized that she had heard a faraway sound that might have been a car door closing, and went out into the hall. The outside lamp lit, the door open on darkness—and nothing but a lawn full of thronging shadows, and the bleak chafing wind in the bushes and the leafless trees.

At twenty minutes of nine Victoria paced the living room, fighting for control, keeping back tears of anger and frustration and sudden hollow fear. How unquestioningly she had accepted the telephone message, how quick she had been to read reassurance into an utterly strange voice. Had the call really been from Lilac at all? Or had she herself been decoyed into exactly what she was doing now—putting on her coat, fumbling for the flashlight on the shelf in the closet, following the still restless Saint Bernard out into darkness?

Shandy disappeared into shadows at the end of the lawn. With the flashlight beam playing ahead, Victoria crossed wet grass, went up the driveway to the road and walked a little way along it, listening to the crisp click of her heels on asphalt, hearing nothing else except the small background noises of the night: the tiny creak of tree branches, the occasional stir of a bush, the distant rattle of Shandy's collar. Simon would drive along here shortly, expecting Lilac to answer his knock at the door. She could at least spare him that; Victoria turned back.

Shandy refused amiably to respond to her whistle. He stood motionless in the driveway, plumed tail drooping, white-blazed muzzle pointed at the garage. All at once he made a prancing dash forward on pebbles, then gazed soberly and pleadingly at Victoria.

She came slowly and reluctantly, remembering the far-off suggestion of a car door closing, remembering too that Lilac's convertible had been taken out once before, on Sunday afternoon. But no one would dare take it again when the police had examined it, would be alert for any reappearance of the car.

The garage door slid back with a soft grumble. The car was there; Victoria swung the flashlight in an inquiring gold arc, moving toward the door, calling Shandy in a crisp voice that echoed back to her from cement and brick.

Shandy was whining at the narrow door at the far end of the garage. It opened, Victoria recalled, on an amateur darkroom where Lilac's father had developed and printed endless rolls of film from small mistreated cameras. Because the room had been so long unused, because Shandy had lifted a huge paw and was preparing to assault the door, her voice was sharp with tension. "Shandy! Here, boy. . . ."

She saw it a moment later, the merest half-moon of dark fabric edging from under the door. It looked like the tip of a glove. Victoria straightened, holding herself taut against a dizzying wash of terror. She thought, I can't open the door. I must, and put out a hand and gave a sudden wrench at the knob before panic could put her to flight.

The body that had been flung into the darkroom was

wedged in the narrow aisle between wide shelves and a
table that held an enlarger. It wore a black coat with an
elderly fur collar; one queerly doubled leg showed inches
of sober black ankle. Victoria steadied herself against the
door frame and tried to stop staring at the dark runnel of
blood on Lilac Thall's narrow white face. She didn't realize
until moments had passed that the dog beside her was
quiet, that the whimpering sound in the dim garage was is-
suing from her own sick throat.

CHAPTER 10

THE police. A doctor, if only to straighten the pitiful crumple of bone and flesh. Or—

Was Lilac dead?

Moving stiffly, Victoria forced herself to kneel and find a still-warm hand, to probe with shaking inexpert fingers for a pulse in the limp wrist. For agonized seconds there was only the racketing thump of her own heartbeats, and then she felt it—the delicate stir of life in the motionless body of the girl at her feet.

The next few minutes went in capsuled panic. She was on her feet and running through darkness, phoning a startled operator for police and an ambulance. The thought of Lilac lying unprotected on the darkroom floor sent her flashing back to the garage.

The Saint Bernard was still there, patient and baffled, nosing interestedly at the hem of the dusty black coat. Victoria found the light switch and flipped it on, dissolving the nightmare dimness. How long before the ambulance would arrive? She didn't dare move Lilac; she took off her coat and slid folds of it gently under the glossy dark head. Impossible not to see the deep blood-blurred wound toward the back, not to realize that the milky gleam in one spot was exposed bone— Victoria looked away again, tightening her throat against rage and nausea.

Headlights at last, a car door slamming, footsteps echoing harshly on pebbles in the driveway—she sprang to her feet in relief and ran blindly for the dark mouth of the garage and found herself being steadied in Simon Halliday's arms. "Victoria! What—"

Victoria stopped shaking. She said, "It's Lilac. She's not dead. She's—" and told him. Far away, underlining the words she tried to keep rational, a siren began to rise.

Simon went to the darkroom and bent. He touched Lilac's hand and brushed hair away from the blood on her face and took a long look at the wound on her head. He straightened then, staring down, and spoke almost to himself. "William Fowler. I wonder. . . ."

The siren was closer, ripping through the night not more than a quarter of a mile away. Victoria said incredulously, "William Fowler? But he can't be here; they've been combing the town for him. . . ."

Simon didn't answer. The preoccupied expression left his face and competence came back; he held Victoria's eyes with his own narrow bright gray gaze. "You'd better not tell the police that Lilac called—there'd be hell to pay because they weren't told. You were out with Shandy and he started sniffing around the garage. You—"

The siren had stopped. There were more cars in the driveway, and voices and running men and someone shouting. "In here." Simon said rapidly under his breath, "Stick to that, Victoria," and moved away.

A doctor was followed by interns with a stretcher. One of the interns said, "Can we get that car out of here?" A patrolman produced the extra key to the convertible and backed it out, and more men crowded into the garage. No one paid any attention to Victoria. She stood rigidly apart from the murmuring group gathered around the doctor and watched between overcoats as he listened to Lilac's heart, bared her arm, used a hypodermic and straightened, motioning to the interns. Sergeant Tansill said bluntly, "What about it, doctor?" and he shrugged. His noncommittal "Maybe" struck at Victoria like a blow.

Inch by inch, with incredible tenderness, Lilac was shifted to the stretcher in her incongruous disguise of elderly mourning—black coat and thick black stockings, sedate Cuban-heeled shoes. Without makeup her narrow still face looked pale and defenseless, made chalkier by the disordered black bangs and the long stripe of dried blood.

It was when they lifted the stretcher carefully that she spoke, in a tired dry whisper that was more electrifying than a scream in the damp cement room full of raw white light and waiting men. She said, "I didn't. I didn't. Hope . . ." and moaned a little and slipped into unconsciousness again.

Twenty minutes later, in the living room of the Thall house, Sergeant Tansill listened without comment to Victoria's explanation of how she had discovered Lilac. His face was sombre, his gaze in-turned. He had withdrawn the protective presence of the policeman who might have prevented the nearly fatal attack, and now he seemed possessed by a cold grim anger. Two patrolmen burst into report breathlessly that there was no one around the grounds; Tansill nodded absently without looking up and continued to watch Victoria. When she had finished he nodded again, glanced at his watch and went into the library to telephone.

He was expressionless when he returned. "Didn't you find it rather difficult, Miss Devlin, exercising a dog in those clothes?"

Victoria glanced down with a feeling of unreality at her incisively straight skirt, the tall slender heels of her navy pumps. Even now control came with an effort. "I did, rather. But I was counting on only a week-end, Sergeant, and I brought very little with me in the way of a wardrobe."

"Imagine so. And you'd packed everything else, hadn't you? When had you planned to leave, Miss Devlin?"

Her suitcase and hat and gloves—she'd thrust them into the darkened library before Freddy Spencer arrived. She had forgotten all about them, and Simon hadn't known she intended to leave Seacastle as soon as Lilac was safely home. Be bold about it; Victoria lifted her eyes coolly and said, "In the morning. I supposed that with Lilac presumed drowned, there wasn't much use in my staying on any longer. If she's going to be all right, will there be any objection to my going back to New York?"

"I wouldn't pick an early train," said Sergeant Tansill smoothly. "We'll see what, if anything, Miss Thall can tell us. Meanwhile, there'll be a man outside until morning. I'll be getting along now."

After he had gone, Victoria made coffee and brought it into the living room. Incredibly, it was not quite ten o'clock, only a little over an hour since she had first put on her coat and followed Shandy out into the darkness. Lilac had been taken to Bridgewater Hospital, five miles to the south; Simon was there and would call when there was news.

"I didn't. I didn't," Lilac had whispered insistently. And then, "Hope—" Was it just the word itself, a noun or a verb she had been too weak to amplify? Of course; it had to be. And yet, because of days and nights of tension and wonder, Victoria's mind began to play with the single cryptic syllable, turning it this way and that with the too-alert scrutiny that had become habit. Lilac had said, "I didn't." Wouldn't she logically have continued, "I hope—"? It was noun, verb—and name. Somewhere, at some time, Victoria had known a girl called Hope. Lilac had known her too . . . where, when? Victoria, trying for the careless detachment that spurs recollection, remembered all at once.

Carmichael, Hope Carmichael. Butter-yellow curls went with it, and a cloying Carolina accent. Hope Carmichael had been the Southern belle of the class at Miss Harvey's Academy.

She began to roam the room, forgetting her untouched cup of coffee. Hope Carmichael and Lilac's stolen diary for the year 1941—both linked with the Boston boarding-school she and Lilac had attended together. Something had happened that year, then, and its echoes still sounded in Lilac's inexplicable drugging and her desperate trip to New York, in the whole grim plan that had ended in a murderous assault in the dark.

But . . . William Fowler, the prowling and dreadful X. Simon had said his name musingly out there in the garage, and William Fowler could hardly have been further removed from a finishing school for Boston young ladies.

Her coffee was cold, but she drank it without noticing and lighted a cigarette. It was better to concentrate like this, to try not to think of Lilac balancing delicately between life and death. Think instead of Hope Carmichael, who boasted drawlingly of her beaux and her blue-blooded Carolina forebears, who hinted tantalizingly that she had been sent north to school because of Trouble with Men. What connection could Hope have now with Lilac? At Miss Harvey's she had had her own admiring coterie; Lilac and Victoria had looked on her with dislike and a touch of reluctant awe. Had Lilac, in spite of it, kept in touch with her all these years?

Hope would be married now; she wasn't a girl, Victoria thought, who would willingly have breakfasted alone after the age of eighteen. But what memory did Lilac share with her, so strongly that her name might have come to Lilac's lips in delirium? There were other girls called Hope, of course. But there was also the missing diary for that same elusive year.

It was close to eleven o'clock before Simon called from the hospital in Bridgewater. Lilac had come down from the operating room without recovering consciousness; no one had been allowed to see her and there was a police guard outside her room. Millicent Spencer was there but was leaving shortly; Grace Halliday and Olive and Rufe had all wanted to drive immediately to the hospital but Sergeant Tansill had advised against it.

Simon's voice over the telephone was tired and empty. "So that's that. I'm getting chased out of here myself, so there's nothing much for me to do but come home and wait for them to call. But I'd like to talk to you first."

To be alone with Simon again, feeling as she felt ... "I don't think you'd better tonight," Victoria said steadily. "Everything's all right here. And you ought to get some sleep if they're going to phone you later."

There was a pause. "Maybe you're right," said Simon distantly, and said good-night and hung up.

Victoria went woodenly upstairs with her suitcase, fumbled through it for a toothbrush and nightgown and lay for a long time staring at darkness. Lilac must live; she said it fiercely over and over in her mind as though by sheer will she could get through to the mysteriously sleeping brain of the girl in the hospital. Only if Lilac lived could she ever shake off the bitter weight of guilt, ever look at herself without horror again.

Because she had agreed to come here at all, and therefore set off this frightful chain reaction. Because, having come, she had fallen in love with the man whom Lilac was to marry.

Because, expressly against Lilac's instructions, she had told Simon of Lilac's impending return to Seacastle, and by doing so had gambled with a life as carelessly as with a flipped coin.

Someone found out, thought Victoria, hearing the

grandfather clock in the library begin the slow strokes of midnight; something about Simon's voice, his bearing, gave away the fact that Lilac was still alive.

William Fowler, then, had slipped completely out of her consciousness.

". . . think she's going to be all right," said Grace Halliday's warm rich voice over the telephone. "It's so hard to be sure with head wounds, of course, but Dr. Lemon was with her most of the night and again this morning. The police haven't been allowed near her—apparently she's conscious only at intervals, and then frightfully weak and wandering. I suppose it's a miracle she's alive at all."

Lilac was going to recover. Days and nights of terror cancelled out in a wink of time; Victoria looked with sudden delight at a sour glitter of sunlight on the library desk and heard herself murmuring into the phone. At the other end of the wire Grace went on; "Simon drove over to the hospital at six this morning—he's just back and I've made him take a sleeping pill, poor dear. I won't have him subjected again to that horde of reporters. . . ."

Victoria thanked her for calling, hung up and stayed indecisively at the phone. There would be reporters, of course, and photographs of the garage with dotted lines and arrows drawn in, and someone would almost certainly try to cajole Shandy into re-enacting the door-sniffing sequence of the night before. Perhaps if she saw Sergeant Tansill or Chesterton in time she'd be allowed to go back to New York.

There was no use now in her staying. Even if Lilac were unable to identify her assailant, she would have to explain her theoretical disappearance on Sunday night—and the police would undoubtedly talk to her before anyone else could.

Millicent called while Victoria was still standing at the phone. She was, she said, nearly dead with sleep; she'd waited up until nearly four that morning for a call from the hospital. She insisted on hearing in detail what Victoria had already told the police, and interrupted, marvelling, to say, "Weren't you terrified, Victoria, that that lunatic might have been lurking around afterwards? Just think! . . . It's amazing, isn't it, that you should have been out with the dog at just that time?"

Was there shrewdness behind Millicent's innocent patter? Victoria said guardedly that her discovery had been very luckily timed, and Millicent rushed on.

"Those clothes, Victoria! Of course, Lilac's never been any Paris import, but that coat, and those unutterable stockings—where do you suppose she found such frights?"

Where indeed? Second-hand shops, possibly, but the clumsy disguise hadn't worked. Victoria said, "I've no idea, but I suppose Lilac will explain everything herself."

"Yes—after leading us all a merry chase," said Millicent sharply. "Well, I won't keep you. I suppose you'll be busy posing for newspaper photographers."

Victoria ignored that. She said with casual boldness, "By the way, Millicent, I've been wondering—that Mr. Fox who called the other morning when I was at your house sounded rather familiar. Did I ever meet him?"

The wire was silent for a moment; Victoria could almost see the small soft fingers tightening on the receiver as they had tightened so spasmodically on the banister that other morning. Then Millicent said, blundering a little in her haste, "Meet him? Oh, no, I'm quite sure you never did, Victoria. It's only lately that ... he's Freddy's friend, really. There's someone at the door, so I've got to run ... good-bye."

Another man in Millicent's life? Victoria put the phone down. Hardly; quite apart from moral issues Millicent was too cautious, too jealous of her own small comfortable horizon. Why, then, was the mysterious Mr. Fox lying about in her life like an unexploded bomb?

There were only two reporters with Sergeant Tansill and Chesterton when they arrived at nine-thirty; the others, Victoria supposed, were at Bridgewater Hospital waiting for a statement from Lilac Thall. Sitting in the library, with Chesterton watching her out of polite tired eyes, she repeated what she had told Sergeant Tansill the night before.

"And you heard no sounds, nothing at all of the attack on Miss Thall?"

The faraway metallic clip that had roused Shandy—she'd forgotten that. "I heard something that might have been a car door closing. That was at a little after eight, I think. It sounded as though it came from the direction of the road."

Chesterton nodded and made a note. He said abruptly, "Miss Devlin, have you any idea of what Miss

Thall could have been referring to last night when she said 'I didn't, I didn't?'"

"I'm afraid not."

"Would you know of a friend of Miss Thall's named Hope, by any chance, Miss Devlin?"

This was important, she knew it instinctively. But the name had been wrung from Lilac in half-consciousness, and it was only fair to let her deal with it as she pleased when she was out of danger and had had time to think. "Not unless it was someone at school," said Victoria carelessly.

Chesterton turned to Sergeant Tansill and smiled faintly and turned back to Victoria. "I think it's fairly certain that what Miss Thall meant to say was 'I hope.' The sergeant and I have been arguing about that—and he was there, of course. I just wanted to get your opinion. . . ."

He was rising. Victoria said with a faint echo of last night's fear, "But Lilac can tell you herself, can't she?"

"Presumably. But not until she's in shape to talk, and that may be several days."

He was going to leave. Victoria asked if, under the circumstances, there was any reason why she shouldn't return to New York, temporarily at least, and had the impression of a question and answer contained in a single glance between Chesterton and Tansill. Then Chesterton said smoothly, "I understand, Miss Devlin. If you'll just give us your address, in case anything should come up . . ."

She was free. She could leave openly, with official permission, and there was no reason at all to feel a lingering wariness, like a mouse in the face of the cat's sudden lethargy. Victoria called Millicent, said she would leave the house key in the base of the lantern outside the front door, and explained her hasty departure. "I hadn't expected to be away so long, of course, and among other things there's the small matter of rent."

"I know, dear. You've been such a help, I don't know what we'd all have done without you." Millicent sounded silky with relief. "You'll come for the wedding, of course?"

The wedding. The ring, the vows, the soaring, cutting happiness all around her . . . "If I possibly can," Victoria said lightly. "I'll be in touch with Lilac in any case. Goodbye, Millicent."

Twenty minutes later, Shandy was out of the cab with a scrambling bound when they stopped in front of the Hal-

liday house, serene and white and green-shuttered under
leafless elms. Victoria asked the driver to wait, turned to
open the low white gate and collided with a woman who
had just stepped through it. She said, retreating, "I beg
your pardon—" but the woman had brushed impatiently
past her, leaving an impression of a tight colorless mouth
and pears of orange rouge on white cheeks and tightly
waved straw-yellow hair under a black hat.

Victoria let the gate swing to behind her and looked
back. The woman was walking briskly, almost furiously
away, her heels hitting the sidewalk in quick hard snaps,
her shoulders back under a short muskrat coat.

Shandy was pawing and whining at the panelled door.
Victoria dismissed the woman from her mind and started
up the path. A movement in a second-floor caught her eye,
and she glanced up. The face left the window then, and she
was aware that it had been there all the time, as she
climbed out of the cab, as the woman in the muskrat coat
blundered against her and then walked away.

The maid let her in. Rufe was in the hall almost at
once, taking her hand, noting her veil and gloves and crisp
look of departure. "Victoria! Not going back already?"

She had to, Victoria told him, standing in the hall;
there were things to be attended to in New York, and as
she couldn't see Lilac in any event she had better be on her
way. "Thanks very much for Shandy—he's a wonderful
companion."

"Like a tidal wave," Olive said dryly at Rufe's shoulder. "Oh—are you going, Victoria? I wish Aunt Grace
were here to say good-bye, but she's lying down. In fact—"
the feathery no-colored brows drew together in a little
frown, "there was someone here to see her just a few
minutes ago, but I didn't dare wake her. She gave Simon a
sleeping pill and then took one herself, and they're both
dead to the world."

If they were, thought Victoria fleetingly, then someone
else had been standing at an upstairs window staring down
with that peculiar air of intentness, watching the swift and
angry departure of the woman in the muskrat coat.

But all that was over and done with, the wondering
and the secret surveillance and the amorphous fear that refused, somehow, to solidify itself into the shape of William
Fowler. Lilac was in safe and sterile hospital hands now,
under the protection of the police. Any threat, any linger-

ing trace of menace would be blotted up by their combined watchfulness.

Three-quarters of an hour later, Victoria was on the train for New York.

CHAPTER 11

IT WAS odd to wake again to the rushing rhythm of traffic below her on the other side of the court. Victoria lay startled and half-asleep, listening to the call of a horn, the clopping of a horse's hoofs, a truck delivering coal somewhere. She thought, I ought to be up in case the phone rings, and realized with her cheek still warm against the pillow that it was Friday; that she was no longer in Seacastle, that there was no urgent message to wait for. And no one in New York knew she was back.

It was a wonderfully free-agent feeling. She lingered in the shower, brushing her hair before the steamy mirror and actively enjoying the thunderous sound of the Van Horn children in the apartment over hers. The distantly thudding shower was Mr. Van Horn's; in exactly twenty-five minutes he would be riding down in the elevator, blond and handsome, smelling amiably of aftershave lotion. This was routine. This was *safe*.

Then why was there that faint persistent shadow, as annoying as a blind spot in an otherwise clear mirror? It was, of course, the feeling that somehow and at the end she had failed Lilac. But that was nonsense, Victoria told herself, turning bacon in the apartment's tiny kitchen. Lilac would see the newspapers, and Victoria's story was there in detail; she needn't be trapped into lies over that part of it.

For the rest ... what else could she have done, with a police guard outside Lilac's hospital room, with Sergeant Tansill and Chesterton and the Hallidays hovering like hawks? Pouring coffee, looking down at a catalpa in the court below, Victoria began to put the past six days determinedly behind her.

Her life was here, to be taken up when she wanted. There was accumulated mail: two bills, a note from the Meads asking her to a cocktail party on Sunday, a birth announcement, a cordial letter mentioning an interview from one of the editors of *Vogue*, a pencilled list of notations from Jim Patterson, beginning on last Saturday with a sad, "Came and you were out; will call," and ending yesterday morning with an outraged, "Where the hell are you?" Victoria smiled, looking at the scribbled messages. She liked Jim Patterson; for the past year, in fact, their relationship had been drifting toward the inevitability of marriage. He was clever and attractive, gay when you wanted him to be and sensitively quiet when you weren't in the mood for wit. Patient as Jim had been, he would want to know soon how she felt about spring weddings. Very fine, thought Victoria, staring with sudden bleakness at sunlight on the floor. A lovely time of year to be married. But not for me, thank you.

It was almost possible all that morning and afternoon to forget that she had ever left this urban existence. She telephoned her Aunt Ellen, who considered newspapers too depressing to read these days and consequently knew nothing about the Seacastle murders, and agreed to lunch at one o'clock. After lunch she spent a lazy two hours on Fifth Avenue, buying gloves and an extravagant hat, having a silver rattle sent to the Metcalfes' new baby. The first thin shadow of dusk was in the streets and the wind was sharpening when she succumbed to a dozen buttery daffodils in the florist's shop on the corner and turned into her own apartment building.

Call Lilac tonight; when that was done the last tie would be cut. Victoria bought a newspaper from the elevator boy and went into her apartment, lighting lamps, putting the daffodils in a bowl on her bookcase, sitting down at last with a cigarette and the paper.

She found it on page seven, a scant three inches of type that said, "Seacastle, Mass.—Police are awaiting positive identification of a body believed to be that of William

Fowler, 33, escaped paranoiac from Bellemarsh Sanitarium, for whom police of three states have been searching in connection with the murders of Louise Brainard, Elizabeth Cossett, and Alma Corey, Boston nurse. The body, half-buried in mud in a lonely section of marsh, was found by a sixteen-year-old boy. . . ."

Victoria let the paper fall. She thought with an odd feeling of disbelief, It's finished. William Fowler must have come back to the Thall house for something, and ran into Lilac in the dark and got frightened and fled again, and somehow . . . What? Suicide? Or an accidental killing in the windy black night by someone who didn't dare come forward?

There were curiously few details. Victoria opened the paper again and went back over the bare account. A boy rescuing drifted lobster traps had caught a glimpse of something bright under piled brush and damp shingles. It was the blade of a sickle. A few feet away he had found a man's body face down in the mud, and had then called police from the nearest house. . . .

Piled brush and shingles. Had someone tried deliberately to hide William Fowler's body—and in heaven's name, why? Victoria folded the paper with a decisive crackle and was warmly, abruptly grateful for her small safe apartment, for rush-hour traffic echoing dimly up from the street and endless gold windows poised against the night sky.

The phone rang. It would be Jim, or possibly Eleanor Mead. In the bedroom Victoria lifted the receiver and said expectantly, "Hello?"

No one answered. But there was a silent, breathing presence on the line; she said to it impatiently, "Hello? Who—?" and realized that now she was speaking to a dead blank void. At the other end, with a gentle click, someone had hung up.

It had been a wrong number, of course, and the caller hadn't bothered to apologize. Two days ago she would have turned chilly with fear, thinking that someone had chosen an anonymous way of finding out that she was there, and vulnerable.

And it was, after all, only sensible for any girl living alone in New York to fasten the door chain and pull down the Venetian blinds.

It was pleasant to face an idle evening. Tomorrow she

would get in touch with her friends again; tonight she would have a light early dinner, call Bridgewater Hospital and go to bed with a long and soothing book. She had put the telephone call completely out of her mind and was busy with salad when the buzzer rang.

There went her solitary evening, unless she could get rid of whoever it was. Victoria pressed the button that released the downstairs lock, turned off the gas under mushroom soup and opened the door moments later to Simon Halliday.

One speechless second unfolded like an accordion, and she thought flashingly, Simon here ... damn these slippers ... something's wrong with Lilac. And then Simon was saying mildly, "May I?" and moving past her into the living room.

With the knob of the closed door cold and solid in her hand, Victoria found command of herself again. She said coolly, "I'm sorry— I was expecting someone else. Sit down, won't you, Simon? Is there something the matter? Lilac isn't—worse?"

Simon didn't move. He stood still with his hat in his hand, too tall for her oyster and blue and green room. He was frowning a little. "You left so suddenly. When I woke up they said you'd come and gone."

"I wanted to get an early train. I'd been away too long as it was, and they wouldn't let me see Lilac anyway ... how is she, Simon?"

"She won't be out of the hospital for a while," Simon said carefully. He glanced around the room and then back at her face. "Did you know you were being watched, Victoria?"

"Then you shouldn't have come. They'll think—" She had spoken before she thought, and she could feel her face burning as she walked quickly past him and bent her head to light a cigarette. The words finished themselves in her mind: They'll think you show too much interest in me for a man who's engaged to be married, whose fiancée is desperately ill. They'll remember that we were out driving together on the night Nurse Corey was murdered, and that you were with me in the garage when the ambulance came for Lilac. . . . She said suddenly, "Did you call me an hour or two ago?"

"No. I found your address in a phone book at the airport and came straight here. I suppose it didn't occur to me that you wouldn't be in."

He had sat down at last. Victoria was appalled to realize that it was natural and dangerously nice to have him there on her couch, that after the first shock she accepted his presence gladly and without question. Her voice, asking if he would like a drink, was scrupulously remote.

She could hear him moving restlessly about as she took out ice and bitters and rye; he was touching her books, flipping through the pages of the magazine she'd worked for until a few weeks ago, examining a small etching between the windows. She called, "What makes you think I'm being watched?" and he was in the kitchen, taking the drink from her hand.

"I dropped in at the police station and overheard the end of a telegram Tansill was sending to New York," he said. "He's being quite polite about it, but I gather he's rather interested about your fingerprints. He and Chesterton were unbosoming themselves while I was waiting to see him. Apparently there were some diaries of Lilac's——"

Of course. Her fingerprints had been on those, and on the fender of Lilac's car, and on the garage door. And she had been alone in the house when Lilac was attacked, she had entered the house alone, earlier, on the night Nurse Corey was murdered. Perhaps they had traced the long-distance call with the message that Lilac was coming back. . . . Fear touched Victoria and slid away again. She said, "But that man they found—wasn't it William Fowler after all?"

"Yes. It was Fowler all right."

"Then why. . . ?"

"He'd been dead nearly two weeks," said Simon bluntly, looking at her out of direct gray eyes. "He killed the Brainard child and the librarian—they found evidence of that. But he couldn't have killed the nurse, Miss Corey, and he didn't attack Lilac."

Dead nearly two weeks—the dreadful implications of that were slow in focussing. "Was he killed?" asked Victoria numbly. "Or did he drown, or what?"

"He committed suicide." Simon's voice was flat. "There's apparently no doubt about that at all. He used the sickle, and from the general set-up the police are certain that he did it himself. The police think someone passed by on the road bordering the marsh, and he went crazy all over again with the fear of capture. Anyway, the next morning, before it was light, a lobsterman that lives down there dumped a lot of brushwood and stuff in just that spot, intending to burn it when it got dry enough. He never did get around to burning it, but it covered Fowler's body all that time. That's how they can place the time of death so accurately."

William Fowler was dead, and nothing was solved at all. Victoria felt sick at the inescapable conclusion. "Then someone else used a sickle to kill Nurse Corey because—"

"Because if and when they took William Fowler alive, who'd believe he'd killed two woman and not three? The details were all in the papers at the time—helpful, wasn't it?" said Simon grimly. "The one thing someone didn't count on was that he was dead at the time he was supposed to have killed the nurse. So in a way I'm an advance guard—this is where the police come in, instead of step out."

Victoria didn't ask what he meant; she knew, coldly and without doubt. The Thall family was Nurse Corey's only tie with the seacoast town where she had been murdered—and through Lilac Thall the people with whom she had come in contact that week-end: the Hallidays and Olive Stacey, Millicent and Freddy Spencer, Victoria herself. One of them had read the newspaper accounts of those two other deaths, one of them had quietly and murderously chosen a sickle from the shed at the Thall house and coaxed Nurse Corey into the fatal dark. One of them must have been serenely amused about the furore over William Fowler's supposed third victim. . . .

The realization made a blurred and hideous montage for Victoria. Traffic, reassuring lights, her own cool, gay serene living room gave way to a delicately sinister scene. Someone watching, planning, coming quietly to the shed at the back of the Thall house. Victoria and Nurse Corey moving confidently about only a wall's thickness away—while known fingers closed over a sickle's handle, while a familiar shape crept out into the darkness again. . . . It was someone, she faced it coldly, to whom she had spoken words of reassurance about Lilac. Someone who had pretended worry and solicitude, and had waited only for the chance to strike another killing blow. . . .

The black scene dissolved; there was Simon's narrow thoughtful face and inquiring eyes. Victoria said dispassionately, "I'm surprised, under the circumstances, that the police haven't sent for me."

Simon shrugged and nodded at the windows. "After all, they know where you are. I imagine you'll get a call tomorrow. Meanwhile, I thought— I didn't want you to have all this sprung on you out of the blue."

The voiceless telephone call, then, had been the detective or policeman who was shadowing her; he had lost her temporarily and had checked her apartment, not bothering with a wrong-number pretense. The small relief Victoria felt vanished under the implication of what Simon had just said. He was warning her, giving her time to think—did he actually suspect her of Nurse Corey's murder, of the attack on Lilac?

He was looking at his watch, saying almost to himself, "There's a plane I can get—" and then glancing up at her. "The family think I'm at a business dinner in Hartford— I've squared that with a fellow I know there. That's in case the police drop by. And Victoria . . ." His eyes were incredibly like Rufe's, she thought, gray and compelling and darkly lashed, with an odd hazel ring around the iris. "Stick to the dog-walking story on the night Lilac came back. You'd no earthly reason to harm her, God knows, but if they found out you knew exactly when she was coming they'd fasten on that."

Victoria stared her bewilderment. She said, "But Lilac—" and then, as the phone rang in the bedroom, "Just a second."

It wasn't the police. Jim Patterson's voice, sounding anxious and relieved at the same time, came over the wire. "I was beginning to think you'd been kidnapped. Your aunt said you were in Boston, but I figured nobody would want to stay in Boston that long. Look, you haven't got your hair in an old stocking or something, have you? Can I come over and get a civil reception?"

This was the dream world, Victoria thought, pulling at tufts on her bedspread; this was someone she had known politely long ago. Had she really been fool enough to think she could slip back into this as though she had never been gone? She heard her own voice with the impatience in it curbed, explaining that she had a headache and was going to bed, that she couldn't have dinner with him tomorrow night. She'd tell him all about it later . . . yes . . . yes . . . nonsense. Good-night.

Simon looked at her oddly when she returned to the living room. "I'm afraid I've disrupted your evening."

"You haven't at all. But you were saying not to mention the phone call, the message Lilac sent. She'll tell the police herself, probably, she'll have to explain those clothes she was wearing. . . ."

She had thought, ten minutes earlier, that she was beyond shock. But she was totally unprepared for the rocking impact of what Simon told her, staring at a point beyond her shoulder, his face a stranger's, his voice leashed and steady.

"Lilac won't explain anything for a while. That's what I've been putting off telling you—that the injury seems to have gone deeper than they thought at first. She knew me, for instance, but not as someone she intended to marry. And about this other business—she doesn't remember anything at all."

CHAPTER 12

"DR. LEMON and Dr. Majeski are with her now. If you'll wait a few minutes I believe you can see her. You're not with a newspaper, are you, Miss—?"

"Devlin. No, just a friend."

The third-floor superintendent smiled confidingly. "You wouldn't believe the trouble we've had with reporters since Miss Thall was admitted. We even had one dressed up as a nurse, but of course we saw through that immediately. There you are. If you'd like to go into that waiting room across the hall . . ."

Victoria took the card the woman handed her, turned into the small bright room and sat down on a chintz sofa. Rubbery feet whisked by the doorway now and then, a tray-laden cart rattled past, a voice around the corner whispered explosively, "... so I said to her, 'Where do you think you are, Madam, the Ritz?' "

Victoria wasn't conscious of any of it; she was hearing, instead, Simon Halliday's voice in the flat and frightful phrases in which, last night in her apartment, he had described Lilac's condition. Stripped of expression, without even the hazy comfort of impenetrable Latin, they had been even more shocking.

"The consensus of opinion at the hospital seems to be that it can't happen but it has. Physically Lilac's doing very

103

well, no pressure on the brain, nothing you could put on a chart. In fact, they think it's a good idea for her to have visitors, people she knows well, for a few minutes at a time. But the period of amnesia or whatever they call this seems to go back in spots for a couple of months. It's nothing she's aware of herself, so she doesn't make any effort to remember. It's as though she's—happier with things as they stand. Of course, Lemon isn't a brain man. But Majeski is."

He had glanced at her face then, and read the thought that flashed into it. "They've a brain man coming down from Springfield, and a police alienist from New York. Lilac's polite and cooperative, but quite disinterested about the whole business."

Could she hold a pose of indifference if she were shamming? Victoria twisted her gloves in damp hands and looked out at chilly glass-gray sky. Sergeant Tansill had been casual on the telephone at nine this morning. Miss Thall hadn't been able to tell them anything as yet, and the District Attorney's office was anxious to get the case cleared up as soon as possible. As Victoria had been at the Thall house during the time of Lilac's disappearance and the attack on her, it would expedite matters if she could return for a few days. . . .

Nothing about Nurse Corey's murder—but then, as Simon had pointed out, the truth about that hadn't been given to the newspapers. There had been pressure and strong criticism over the handling of the Fowler escape as it was, and the longer it could be assumed that the menace had died with him, the better. When Nurse Corey's real killer was exposed, it would be a redeeming feather in the official cap. . . .

Two doctors strolled slowly into view at the doorway. Victoria recognized Lemon, the doctor who had accompanied Lilac to the hospital; the other, then, must be Majeski. She stood up and put out her just-lighted cigarette. The two men moved on, but not before she had heard Dr. Majeski say musingly. "Most unusual. A severe shock earlier might possibly account for it. I remember an instance . . ."

The third-floor superintendent was in the doorway. "All right, Miss Devlin. Just a few minutes, now—and you won't excite her in any way, will you? Dr. Lemon is very anxious . . ."

And Victoria, her heart beating thickly, paused a moment in the door of Lilac's room and closed the retreating footsteps away.

This was the moment for which she had waited so long, the point toward which she had counted first days and then hours and minutes. Here, certainly, was the answer to Nurse Corey's murder, here were the shadowy motives that Lilac had locked so secretly away from everyone. And, mockingly, mislaid the key herself.

She lay nearly flat in the high white bed. She had been staring at the ceiling when Victoria entered; she turned her bandaged head slowly and cautiously. "Hello, Victoria. It's nice of you to come."

Victoria went to the side of the bed and took the lifted hand that touched her own and moved nervously back to the coverlet. She said, "How do you feel, Lilac?" Against her will her voice came out stiltedly, in a fragile hospital hush.

"Quite well, thanks." Lilac didn't smile. "There's a chair over there."

She was thinner. She looked, Victoria thought, covering shock, infinitely strange, as though the contours of her face had altered subtly to harbor a new and different identity. She had put on a little lipstick, and against it her skin was luminously white, her long gray eyes so bright they looked almost lacquered. But she had no fever, the hand under Victoria's had been cool and dry.

"Thank you for the flowers," said Lilac, still in that curiously aloof voice. "I'm being rather a nuisance to everyone, I'm afraid. I ought to have had a flashlight with me, of course."

Victoria held her breath. Lilac was remembering the attack in darkness, the silent and murderous blow that, aimed a little differently, would have killed her. She sat motionless in the small armchair, concentrating on a fold of the crinkled white bedspread, waiting.

"I suppose I tripped," said the voice from the bed. "That spot in the driveway that's always needed filling—I must have that taken care of as soon as I get home. Smoke if you feel like it, Victoria—it doesn't bother me at all."

She had dismissed the incident. It was incredible. Victoria took a cigarette from her bag and wondered, appalled, what it must mean to have your memory supplying only a blur where there should be sharply-focussed detail.

It must, she thought, be rather like gazing squarely into a mirror and seeing no reflection at all.

It didn't seem to worry Lilac. Her upturned face expressionless on the pillow, she was staring again at the ceiling. Victoria looked at her and at the closed door, and drew in a long breath. She said casually, "Did you have a successful trip, Lilac?"

The hand nearest Victoria made a small startled movement. Lilac turned her head, frowned with pain and gazed slantingly at Victoria out of shining unreadable eyes. "Trip?" she repeated. "Trip? . . . oh." The wonder went out of her face; Victoria, fascinated and a little frightened, watched it change before her eyes until, for a tiny interval, it was Lilac's own remembered face again.

"It was quite sunny, and I swam a lot, but I didn't enjoy it really," said the girl in the bed. "I couldn't forget— you can't that easily. I even told Nurse Corey, after a nightmare once, but that didn't help either."

This was the trip to Bermuda.

"Told her what, Lilac?" Victoria's voice was easy and gentle, suggesting an answer, not insisting on it. Her breath seemed to have caught somewhere deep in her throat.

"Something frightful," Lilac said. Her face twisted; for an instant she was a terrified child pleading mutely and despairingly for help. "I know what it is and—yet . . . I don't. But it's there, and it won't go away until . . ."

Victoria located the bed cord with her eyes. Don't excite her in any way—but Nurse Corey had been struck down and Lilac had barely escaped with her life. She said softly, "Until when?"

Lilac's face closed abruptly. She turned her head away and resumed her search of the ceiling, her withdrawal so complete that Victoria might already have been on the other side of the door. She said, "Nurse Corey is dead, isn't she?"

"Yes." Had they told her, in an effort to shock her into remembrance, or was it knowledge that had clung somehow, a shred of awareness in surrounding emptiness?

"She's dead because she knew," said Lilac impersonally, without removing her gaze from the ceiling.

"But you're safe now," Victoria said. She had risen and stood beside the bed, her gloves and bag in one hand, the other going reassuringly out to Lilac's. She realized with alarm that the fingers she touched were hot, that the sharply contoured cheeks were beginning to flush. She shouldn't have stirred up fear in Lilac, she had no right to jeopardize the other girl—she jerked at the bed cord in something approaching panic, and Lilac looked up crossly. "There's no need to do that. I was just going to sleep, and now they'll come and stick things in my mouth. Oh, well. Good-bye, Victoria. Thank you for coming."

The third-floor superintendent came in, looked flusteredly at Lilac and turned to Victoria with her mechanical affability gone. "Really, Miss Devlin. I thought you'd left long ago—I was called away from my desk and I trusted to your own good sense. . . ."

"It's all right, nurse," said Lilac from the bed. Her voice sounded tired and innocent. "I'm glad we had a chance to talk—Miss Devlin won't be able to come back soon again."

Hostility under the innocence: "Stay away. I don't want to see you." Was Lilac really frightened of some dreadful memory which she had succeeded in forgetting for the time being? Or was she still playing her stubborn, dangerous game?

Rufe was waiting in the station wagon. Walking swiftly away from the elevator, Victoria brushed past a man standing at the receptionist's desk and talking in a low urgent voice. Because his head was bent and he still wore a gray felt hat, she didn't realize until she stood on the hospital steps outside that it had been Charles Storrow.

Rufe let in the clutch and started down the hospital hill. "How is she?"

"She seems fairly comfortable. She doesn't," said Victoria carefully, "remember anything at all about being attacked."

"Odd," murmured Rufe, his eyes on the road. "I had an impression, probably out of an old Clark Gable movie, that everything came back within a short time after the injury, providing the damage wasn't permanent. You don't suppose she could be—protecting anybody?"

"I doubt it. Would you feel awfully protective toward someone who had just hit you over the head with something heavy?" Over words she hardly heard, Victoria felt the edge of dread. Rufe was only skirting, carelessly, what the police themselves must have already considered—that Lilac would protect Simon, and that Simon had arrived at the Thall house shortly after the attack on her. Only Victo-

ria knew the damning prelude to that. Simon had been expecting Lilac at eight o'clock. Simon could have pulled his
car off the road and waited, and the sound of a metal door
closing might have come after he had bundled an inert
body into the seat beside him. . . .

"Do you mind?" Rufe stopped the car along the edge
of a wide beach. Staring out over tumbling dark gray
waves, he said, "Simon's been acting oddly for the past few
days. Oh, I know he's been half-demented over Lilac, and
that business at the office, but still . . ."

"Is something wrong at the office?"

"They've lost another account. A big one—one of the
mainstays, in fact. The agency that picked it up is the one
Simon worked for before he started his own. Which hardly
looks good, even though it's changed hands since then."

"But certainly no one would think that Simon had
anything to do with losing the account. It's his own agency,
after all—" This wouldn't do, this sudden flare of anger at
any indirect reflection on Simon. Victoria finished more
calmly, "It's rather absurd to think he'd deliberately damage his own interests that way, isn't it?"

"Of course," Rufe said, too quickly. "I'm sure they
never thought seriously for a minute that—"

" 'They?' "

"The other directors." Rufe's narrow nervous fingers
made a broken rhythm on the edge of the steering wheel.
"When the agency was just getting started and the only
mail consisted of bills, Simon managed to sell a lot of
stock. He's still got a controlling interest, of course, but just
about. Not that all this matters. They found the woman responsible for the leakage that's been causing all the trouble.
Pillar of virtue, as usual, who used to be Simon's secretary—at the other agency." He twisted the ignition key. "I
suppose, when you add it all up, that it's enough to make
Simon stalk around like a ghost. . . ."

Victoria had felt a memory stir. A muskrat shoulder
brushing hers, a pale vindictive mouth in an orange-rouged
face, angry footsteps hurrying into the distance. She said
slowly, "Did the secretary—the woman who used to work
for Simon—come to your house the other morning? The
day I brought Shandy back?"

Rufe stared a moment, his hand motionless on the
gear shift. Waves crashed on the beach below them, a gull
whimpered, the car shook faintly under a gust of wind.

The silence was longer and hollower than it should have been.

"Yes, I believe she did at that," Rufe said then, putting the car in motion. He had lowered the window to look out as he backed, and his voice came over his shoulder in fragments. "Recriminations ... promises of reform ... that kind of thing. She did it for her old mother—you know the routine. How much space have I got on that side, Victoria, or can you see ... ?"

Rufe didn't want to talk about the visit of the woman in the muskrat coat. For some reason, Victoria knew as she went upstairs to her room at the East Wind, he had been on the brink of denying that she had been at the house at all.

"You say, Miss Devlin, that Mr. Halliday arrived at the garage on the night Miss Thall was attacked purely by coincidence?"

"Of course."

"Oh. He was in the habit, then, of dropping in during the evening?"

"He'd been kind enough to walk the dog for me once or twice. It was a Saint Bernard, and rather unmanageable."

"But you managed very nicely that night, didn't you, Miss Devlin? In spite of the fact that you were dressed more suitably for—let's say a train trip?"

This was Chesterton, who had changed from quiet tired courtesy to smooth tireless hounding. Even his telephone call to her temporary quarters at the East Wind half an hour ago had had command under a thin surface of guarded politeness. Now, seated opposite him, Victoria forced herself to meet his eyes levelly, willed her traitorously restless hands into stillness, "As I explained to Sergeant Tansill, I had a very limited wardrobe with me."

Chesterton nodded absently, his attention on a small slip of paper on the desk before him. "You received a call from New York on Tuesday evening at the Halliday home, Miss Devlin. Would you mind telling me who that was from?"

Oh, God. Why had she been so stupid, why hadn't she coached Aunt Ellen at lunch yesterday? But there was still the telephone, and the blind chance that her aunt might cover for her automatically.... "Not at all. My aunt, Mrs. Charles Snow."

"I see. You had told her in advance, then, where you would be?"

"No. But she knew the Hallidays were friends of Lilac's, and it was the logical place for her to try when no one answered at the Thalls'."

"Of course. And your aunt's address, and telephone number?"

Victoria's mouth went dry as Chesterton handed the memo to a policeman lounging outside the door. They would find out now that she had lied, and it would be worse than the damaging truth. The policeman went into the outer office and Victoria heard the phone being lifted, the quiet impersonal click of the trap.

"You knew the Thall house quite well, Miss Devlin?"

"Yes." In the background, the policeman's voice completed a Circle number.

"Had you ever noticed that the inside door to the shed was unlocked, although the rest of the house was securely fastened up?"

The shed. Where the sickle had been. But it was locked the last time I looked, Victoria thought; she heard her voice telling Chesterton so, and knew without surprise that someone had deliberately slid the little bolt back to show how easily she, or any other visitor to the Thall house, could have had access to the shed and the weapon. They were going to arrest her; why didn't they do it quickly and get it over with? In the room beyond, the policeman hung up and came to the office doorway. "No answer, sir. I'll keep trying."

No answer. Aunt Ellen, wonderful creature, was out shopping or rapping for order at one of her endless committee meetings. Victoria lowered her lashes over relief and tried to keep her face impassive.

Chesterton eyed her grimly. "Just a few more questions, Miss Devlin...."

A half hour more, while the light at the window grew cold and blue and Victoria began to realize why they had not arrested her. They believed that Nurse Corey's murderer and Lilac's assailant were one and the same person; that, from the very nature of the first crime, the killer must necessarily have had intimate knowledge of how William Fowler's victims had died. Someone who lived in Seacastle, someone who had drawn the essential details from newspapers and rumors and the furtive and terrified grapevine, and had then planned a far more monstrous thing. But—— "held for questioning." The police did that, didn't they, when they weren't satisfied with a witness?

She was out in the street at last. The west was blown and red; looking down a side street Victoria could see a slice of the harbor, the near water cold purple-blue, turning to fiery turquoise where the last of the sunset warmed it. Far out, the sloping shore of Seacastle Point was bathed in sleepy pink light.

Call Aunt Ellen at once, immediately. She would be alarmed and worried and curious, but that couldn't be helped. Victoria opened the door of the drug store, paused, looked at the laughing group of high school students at the counter beside the phone booth and went out again. She couldn't call from there, lifting her voice in piercing long-distance explanations.

The East Wind, where she was staying, was worse. It was a small inn in summer, a private house with rooms for rent in winter. Its sole telephone, in the downstairs hall, was a source of unfailing interest for the three elderly sisters who ran it, as well as for any bored and idle lodger.

The stationery store, then. Time was ticking by; at any moment the policeman in the station three blocks behind her might lift the phone again. Perhaps even now Aunt Ellen was unlocking the door of her apartment . . . hurry.

The booth in the stationery store was occupied. Outside it a waiting woman kept a vigilant patrol, tapping a coin against a table that held a display of greeting cards. Victoria turned despairingly away, feeling as though the very air were hostile.

What else was there? A fish store window with some haddock peering out of cracked ice, Hamilton's Dry Goods, where a wooden child played with a plush dog behind mauve crepe paper and plate glass. Victoria walked briskly on, taking the right hand of the fork that led out of the town, her shoulders taut against bitter sweeping wind. There *was* a phone, in safety and remoteness, if she remembered the address correctly and could find it in what little remained of the daylight. . . .

Five minutes more rewarded her with the small, weather-blurred sign: Blackfan Road. Not a Through Way.

There weren't many houses along here. Victoria walked faster, conscious of the sound of her footsteps in the coming twilight. She passed a small vacant lot with a For Sale notice, a lighted cottage, an amiable black dog, another house with boarded windows. At the end of the lane she paused uncertainly, looked for a mailbox, found it and went up a short brick path.

Charles Storrow wasn't at home; the windows of the neat white house were gray and the only room she could see into lay in dimness. Victoria knocked again, realizing with sharp disappointment how much she had depended on this avenue of escape. A moment later, she blessed Storrow's carelessness with lock and key as the door swung in under her tentative touch.

She stood in a small tidy living room, shadowed in dusk, with the open doorway to the kitchen on her left. A flick of the wall switch brought the room bouncing up into bright emptiness, showed her the telephone on top of a low bookcase across the room. Beside the bookcase was another doorway. Victoria snapped the light off again, took two hesitant steps, called uncertainly, "Mr. Storrow?" and waited.

The tiny repeated sound hadn't come from beyond the doorway after all, it was a miniature splash from a faucet in the kitchen. And there wasn't time to waste now. She might be too late already. Explain to Charles Storrow later; meanwhile, the empty house was a stroke of luck. Victoria lifted the receiver and put it down again in slow, pulsing fear.

There was someone in the room beyond the half-open door.

Seconds ticked by and became an infinite minute before she heard the sound again, a faint sly crackling followed by a curiously muted tap. Nothing after that but her own frightened breathing as she sat moveless in the gloom beside the window with coldness brushing at her.

It took her a few moments to realize that the coldness had a physical source. There was a draft blowing through the open door of the hidden room; it strengthened suddenly and the crackling came again. The wind, thought Victoria with shame and relief. The wind, but still—

Look and make sure, then telephone and leave the neat little house behind her in the dusk. Victoria walked to the door and pushed it wide on a small blue-walled bedroom. The window was open, and the shade cord tapped as she stood there, a crumpled ball of paper went skipping and crackling along the slit between screen and sill.

Charles Storrow was home. He had been home all the time. Peacefully, serenely dead on white candlewick.

Victoria's shaking hand found the door frame and left it again in panic. The footsteps outside were brisk, purposeful. There was someone coming up the little brick path.

CHAPTER 13

VICTORIA didn't consciously plan to hide. She hadn't, until the primitive and violent reaction of nerves and muscles took her there, even noticed the closet in the wall to her right. But she was inside it, with wool against her cheek and a hanger digging into her shoulder, when the front door opened and footsteps came to a sharp stop out in the living room.

"Charles?" It was a woman's voice, breathless and excited. "Charles! Where are you? I've found it. I . . ."

The woman was Olive Stacey. Her voice had come closer until she spoke from the threshold; it stopped as choppily as though a hand had smothered her mouth. For a few eerie seconds there was nothing in the silence but her harsh uneven breathing, and then she took a slow step closer to the bed, said, "Charles?" in a terrified whisper, and left the room rapidly. Her retreating footsteps quickened, the front door closed behind her. Victoria, slipping out of the closet and taking a great dizzying gulp of cool air, reached the living room windows in time to see Olive's tall figure, darker than the twilight, hurrying down the lane at what was almost a run.

She herself had to get away from here quickly, before the police could arrive and find her for the third time at a scene of violence. Violence? However Charles Storrow had

114

died, it hadn't been by physical force. Victoria retrieved her bag from concealing shadows beside the chair on which she had sat, and forced herself to the doorway of the bedroom.

No violence, certainly. The man who had loved Lilac so long and so fruitlessly was stretched on the bed in an attitude only a little more final than complete relaxation. One arm hung over the edge of the bed; it was the ends of the fingers, bent stiffly inwards, that had told her he wouldn't wake again. There was a water glass on the bedside table, and a little bottle lying on its side. The trailing hand hovered over a framed photograph on the floor beside the bed, as though it had slipped from the dying fingers as reluctantly as life had gone out of the body.

Victoria knew what the photograph would be even before she advanced into the blue shadows of the darkening room. The portrait of Lilac, gay and a little mocking, gazed up at her out of its frame for a moment before she turned and fled, running as much from the threat of tears as the queer close presence of death.

She hadn't removed her gloves. Victoria closed the front door soundlessly behind her and went down the brick path in the thickening twilight without looking back at the neat little white house.

Miss Agatha Soames, at fifty-nine the youngest co-proprietor of the East Wind, gazed at the newest boarder with rapt fascination. Sam Shaw, who delivered butter, eggs and gossip every other day, had seen the girl going into the police station on High Street hours ago. And here she was, late for dinner, looking white and shaky and windblown as she closed the front door behind her and started for the stairs.

They grilled her, thought Miss Soames with a half-joyous thrill of horror. What if she really had hit the Thall girl over the head and tried to kill her? Then there was a would-be murderer in the house, and she and Rosie and Hester helpless and unprotected unless you counted old Colonel Masters, who couldn't seem to cope with anything heavier than a small brandy. . . . Good Heavens.

"Miss Devlin," said Miss Soames quaveringly.

The girl hadn't heard; she was starting up the stairs like a sleepwalker, the overhead light making a soft dazzle on her pale wind-brushed hair. "Miss Devlin," said Miss

Soames more loudly, cowering a little in the parlor doorway. "I'm afraid my sisters forgot to tell you—there was a telephone message for you earlier today, about noon I guess, just after you left for the hospital. He didn't leave his name, but he said he was the friend of Miss—Miss Thall's who had called you once about an engagement book. He'd like you to call him back."

She wouldn't have thought it possible that the girl could turn any whiter, but she did. "Like a sheet," said Miss Soames a minute later in the kitchen. "Like a—well, a sheet. And then thanked me and went upstairs without another word. There's something odd about that girl, with the police after her and all. Still, I suppose we ought, somebody ought, to go up and ask her if she'd like some dinner. . . ."

"Not I," said Rosie flatly.

"If she's hungry, she'll follow her nose," said Hester.

"Then I guess I . . . we'll just wait a bit," said Agatha.

Charles Storrow hadn't committed suicide serenely and without fuss in the neat little house on Blackfan Road. In the bedroom upstairs Victoria put her bag and gloves on the bureau, looked mechanically at herself in the greenish mirror and realized with a vague sense of shock that she was only corroborating an earlier thought.

It was too pat. Exit a faithful and hopeless suitor, with a picture of his beloved clutched in his hand. And the crumpled ball of paper that danced on the sill, the try-to-forgive-me, I'll-always-love-you note he hadn't had heart enough to write—no. The glass and vial beside him on the table, the photograph beneath his hand, the unrumpled bedspread on which he lay were the mocking touches of a murderous mind.

Because if Charles Storrow hadn't killed himself when Lilac had been presumed drowned in the harbor, why now, when she was recovering in the hospital?

Because he had suspected, long before the attack on Lilac, that someone had deliberately tried to harm her with drugs. Would he give up so helplessly, loving her as he did, when his point had been drastically proven?

Because, when he left the message for Victoria to call him back, he had had something to tell her. And he hadn't been given the chance.

If only the message had been delivered to her in time.

If only she hadn't walked past him when he was arguing so preoccupiedly with the desk nurse in the hospital lobby. If only ... if only. It wouldn't bring life back to the still figure in the pathetically tidy house.

And yet—how could you persuade a man to take poison or sleeping pills or whatever it had been so quietly and neatly? Just lie down here, my friend, and die. Mind you don't rumple the spread.

She whirled at a soft double-knock on the door, a timid voice calling, "Miss Devlin? I wondered ... will you be wanting dinner?"

"No!" said Victoria, and must have spoken more violently than she intended to judge by the audible gasp and the flurried retreat. Forgetting the frightened Miss Soames, whichever one of them it had been, she began to pace the floor between door and organdy-curtained window. A faucet dripped in the bathroom; she went in to turn it off impatiently and then stand still, staring down at nickel and green-stained enamel.

There had been water dripping slowly and maddeningly in the kitchen in Charles Storrow's house. He wasn't the dripping-faucet kind—the immaculate hearth, the shining ashtrays, the austerely clean bedroom testified to an unusual neatness. Perfectly possible, of course, that in his agitation on returning from the hospital he hadn't noticed the tiny irregular splashing. Equally possible that he had had a visitor who had washed something at the sink—a cup, or a glass—and hadn't turned the faucet completely off.

Why hadn't she looked in the kitchen? If I were doing it, thought Victoria, staring down through the open window at the harbor curling palely onto rocks; if I were doing it, I'd ... horribly, by degrees, a scene began to take place in her mind between Charles Storrow and his murderer.

Charles wouldn't feel cheerful on returning from the hospital—either because he hadn't been allowed to see Lilac or because he had seen her and was aghast at the change in her. The murderer would say quietly, "Why don't you have a drink?" or coffee or tea or sherry. And into that would go the deadly seasoning. Charles would begin to feel queer after a time, and the murderer would show alarm and solicitude; might even, with the connection carefully severed, go through the motions of a call to a doctor. "He'll be right over. He says to lie down meanwhile and take an emetic—I'll fix it for you. Nothing to worry about, just go inside and make yourself comfortable until he comes."

And then the smiling entry, the proffered water glass. "This won't taste very good but it ought to do the trick. The doctor should be here any minute . . ."

Charles, his perceptions dulled, would take the glass and drink another lethal mixture—needlessly concentrated, so that the dregs would stand up to analysis. And then—what? How simple for the murderer to take the framed photograph of Lilac from its place on the bureau, push it into an unresisting hand.

Charles would be in a coma by then, and the photograph would slide from his fingers to the floor. Very little to do now. Press his fingers, perhaps, on the small glass bottle. Wash and dry the cups or glasses used earlier, in too much of a hurry to notice the drip of the faucet; leave the house, slipping unnoticed down the lane past a closed and boarded house, an amiable black dog, a cottage, a vacant lot. Charles Storrow abandoned in his orderly house, dying or already dead, with cold November wind skittering through the window.

Victoria drew breath through a dry throat. It could have happened that way. It must have been something like that, in order to explain the lazy look of peace in a house where a man had been murdered. Unless the plausible, unthinkable thing were true and Storrow had made a romantic moustache-and-melodrama gesture, complete with lover's note and loved one's photograph.

No. Her mind refused it a second time. He had come too close to the truth about Nurse Corey and Lilac, close enough to make his own death necessary. Had he needed one small corroborative detail from Victoria? At any rate he hadn't been quite sure enough to go to the police. . . .

The police.

She had never called her Aunt Ellen, in New York. By this time the police had probably contacted her and received her innocent, flustered denial of a telephone call to her niece in Seacastle. But she could try, there was still one chance in fifty. Moments later she was on the stairs, had passed the three apprehensive faces peeping out of the dim parlor and was closing the front door behind her.

"Going out to meet that man," said Agatha.

"Police want her again, more likely," said Rosie.

"Maybe," observed Hester dispassionately, "she's just remembered her stomach."

Water Street, dipping and curling along the harbor's edge, was dark and nearly deserted, lit at thrifty intervals by dim silvery street-lamps that glowed on narrow uneven sidewalks before yielding to blackness again. Wind sliced between the old houses perched along the water, combing the last dead leaves out of frozen gardens, tossing the lonely echo of the waves up and down the twisting distance.

The Cabot House. There wasn't time now to wait and waver and hold out for seclusion; she would have to make the best of what opportunity she had. The booths, she recalled, were in a corner of the dining room between windows overlooking the harbor. Perhaps the combined sound of the waves and the dinner-hour clatter would drown out what she had to say, or rather shout—her aunt was hard of hearing. Victoria, opening the door between cedars, reflected with grim amusement that there could be unthought-of ramifications in a surreptitious long-distance phone call to a slightly deaf woman, from a town where an unchaperoned phone booth was as rare as a lobster trap on Fifth Avenue.

The Cabot House had only a sparse collection of diners this evening. Victori closed herself into the farthest booth, gave her number, deposited change and waited. The far-off drawling of the telephone in an empty apartment hundreds of miles away had gone on for some time before she realized with a sudden remembering jolt why the police had been unable to contact Mrs. Charles Snow at her home. What had Aunt Ellen said? Something about Long Island and Welsh terriers and an interior decorator, the usual pattering scramble to which Victoria had listened with only half an ear. Concentrating desperately, she made it come back.

"You remember the Clark Goodhues, don't you, dear? She was Emma Monteith, the youngest girl—the one with the nose—and then she married this man Goodhue and what do you think, they're raising Welsh terriers or breeding them or hatching them or whatever it is on Long Island. It must be fairly profitable, because she's had her whole house re-done and is after me to spend a week-end there. Do you think it will rain this week-end, Victoria? I hope not, I always think Long Island is impossible in the rain. . . ."

Ten minutes later her Aunt Ellen was saying fretfully, "But I didn't, dear. How could I, when I didn't even know where you were? Perhaps it's this connection, and I'm not understanding you properly . . ."

"I know you didn't, but you must say you did if they call you. It's very important, Aunt Ellen—I'll explain why when I get back." At a table not far from the booth, a rabbity woman in an electric blue hat had summoned a waiter and was pointing indignantly at what looked like crabmeat salad and then at her own thin throat. The waiter picked up the salad and stirred it suspiciously with a fork. In Long Island Ellen Snow said docilely,

"Very well, dear. I don't know you at all—that's a trifle difficult as your father was my brother—and I never telephoned you in Seacastle. I suppose if it comes to that I didn't have lunch with you at the Plaza yesterday either. . . ."

By the time Victoria had gone over it again she had exhausted her change and the rabbity woman was warily starting on shrimp. But no one had heard, and the telephone message from Lilac was firmly established as a worried call from her aunt. Victoria left the phone booth with a lighter heart and started across the dining room.

It was Millicent's hat that warned her, because Millicent's face was partly hidden as she squeezed lemon on oysters. Freddy Spencer sat opposite her in the booth, the top of his sandy head just showing. As Victoria approached from behind, there was one of those strange barren dining room lulls when forks are suspended, waiters turned to stone, conversation temporarily dead.

Into it Freddy's voice, low and clear, said, ". . . took it like a lamb. I tell you, Millie, there's nothing to worry about. He never suspected. . . ."

And Millicent, conscious of the hush around them, raised her head to give Freddy a furious signalling frown, and saw Victoria walking in sudden blindness past the booth.

"I'm sure it was. . . ." Millicent's voice rose dimly against the resumed pattern of dining room sounds. A second later there was a touch on Victoria's arm and she looked incredulously into Freddy's round bland face. "We thought we recognized you," Freddy was saying with subdued heartiness, "and sure enough. . . . Have you had dinner? No? How about having something with us? We're just starting. . . ."

There was an ugly familiarity to this; Victoria, following Freddy with a sick tight feeling of shock, realized that it was the second time she had been placed in the position of eavesdropper on Lilac's sister and brother-in-law. It wasn't odd, in view of the fact that the Cabot House was Seacastle's only good dining place and its lights among the few to be seen after six o'clock. Nor was it odd that Freddy and Millicent, living only two minutes' walk away, should be habitués. But it meant that whatever they were involved in had reached a stage where fear had made them careless and secrecy had given way to panic. She was at the table, greeting Millicent with the first excuse that came into her head. The Misses Soames were keeping her dinner hot for her and she really couldn't stay. . . .

He took it like a lamb.

"You really should have come to us," Millicent said, her eyes clear and innocent. "We'd love to have you, Victoria, and they say the beds at the East Wind are appalling. Hard as rock."

He never suspected.

"Have you seen Lilac? They had an idea," said Freddy carelessly, "that seeing someone like you—an old friend, you know, not family—might help her remember. Inhibitions and all that. Turned out to be rot, I suppose?"

Now, unmistakably, they were both watching her, Freddy's eyes light and flickering, Millicent's soft and childishly wide.

"It doesn't seem to have helped so far," said Victoria, and made her apologies again and left.

There's nothing to worry about. Could you watch a man die so trustingly and then go out and eat oysters? Poison might be traditionally a woman's weapon, but it was the method fastidious Freddy might choose and use—no mess, no struggling, little if any actual pain. But the sickle that had slashed and mutilated Nurse Corey—could that have been swung in Millicent's little helpless hands, Freddy's soft plump grip?

But someone had struck again and again with the curved and awkward blade. And hadn't been able to use it on Charles Storrow because William Fowler, the shadowy stand-in, was known to be dead.

Victoria hadn't eaten since noon; in a small nearly-empty restaurant up a side street she ordered a sandwich and coffee. Aunt Ellen was taken care of. There was nothing to do now but wait for someone to discover Charles Storrow's body, and hope that Lilac's dark journeying mind would come safely home. She went back to the East Wind, smoked a last cigarette and lay drowsily still, her mind half-hypnotized by the taffeta sound of waves under the window.

Olive Stacey had entered Charles Storrow's house without the ceremony of knocking. She had called "Charles?" with accustomed familiarity. She had had a secret to share with him, so that her impatient footsteps had brought her heedlessly to the bedroom doorway in search of him. She . . .

Victoria's mind drifted, was locked in sleep, emerged into consciousness some time in the night when she turned over in the East Wind's evilly unyielding bed. It was the memory of Olive's voice that roused her, calling urgently through layers of blackness.

"Where are you? I've found it. . . ."

Charles had wanted to know where something was, had said grimly, "It's important to me." Victoria threw off the last shreds of sleep and stared wide-eyed in the dark at the dim blowing shape of the curtains.

Almost certainly Olive had found the suddenly all-important thing—Lilac's green engagement book.

CHAPTER 14

TRADE knowledge for knowledge; Victoria went back to sleep with the thought, woke and bathed and breakfasted with it the next morning. In the East Wind's small rep-and-linoleum dining room she stared unseeingly at a frail powdery old man who watched her raptly over his toast.

Go directly to Olive and match information. It would, of course, mean admitting her concealed presence in Charles Storrow's bedroom. But Olive herself hadn't called the police and therefore wasn't publicizing her own visit; there would certainly have been repercussions by now, nearly ten o'clock on the following morning, if she had. No; Simon's queer, withdrawn thirtyish cousin was for some reason keeping her own counsel.

There was no sign of the elderly Soames trio. Victoria left the dining room and went into the front hall, and stopped with her fingers touching the telephone on the varnished oak table. Better to take Olive as much by surprise as possible. . . .

Slowly, she mounted the stairs.

A great many things happened late that gusty gray morning. There wasn't a photograph of Lilac Thall in the sombre middle-aged black clothes she had worn when they found her, but a conductor on the New York, New Haven and Hartford remembered a woman dressed like that—she

123

had had to throw back her mourning veil to find her ticket—who had boarded the two o'clock train in New York and left it at South Station.

The alienist from New York spent two hours with Lilac, and emerged to report bluntly, "I'd say it's about fifty-fifty. The girl is frightened half out of her wits, and it's perfectly possible that she's set up a protective mental bloc. But she knows a lot more than she's telling."

The specialist from Springfield said, "It's my opinion that . . ." and, when the technical terms were unscrambled, held much the same view: that the amnesia was genuine but the girl was, consciously or sub-consciously, an "uncooperative subject." It was an interesting case, he added cautiously, and he would of course need further study before he could furnish a complete report. . . .

Both men agreed that Lilac Thall was in no condition to be coerced into talking against her will.

Photographs and a description of Lilac were started on their journey among New York Hotels. And Sergeant Tansill went once more over the typed set of notes on the whereabouts of all those people on Wednesday evening between eight and nine o'clock, the time of the attack on Lilac. Find the attacker, Sergeant Tansill thought, and you would uncover at the same time the driving fear or hatred or greed that had killed Nurse Corey.

The notes themselves were not as informative as the impressions that had lodged themselves in the sergeant's mind, surprisingly cynical behind his round provincial face.

The Spencers cancelled each other out. They had had an early dinner, after which the nervous Millicent had dispatched her husband to the Thall house "to see if there was anything they could do." On his return they had played a game of dominoes—"Dominoes? Good God!" Chesterton had commented—and gone to bed. Maybe. The wife would be the motivating force there, Tansill thought; whenever Mrs. Spencer piped, Mr. Spencer would dance.

The Hallidays had also dined earlier than usual, after which Grace Halliday had retired to her room with a book and an aspirin. "Can anyone corroborate that? I'm afraid not, Sergeant; the others were out and the maid's been leaving directly after dinner the last few days to visit her mother in the hospital. . . ." So Mrs. Halliday, to all intents and purposes, had been a free agent during that hour; she had admitted it with a rueful and charming smile—managing, at the same time, a helpless gesture that called attention to her artificial hand.

Olive Stacey had spent dinner and most of the evening at the home of a Mrs. Gordon Kellerman, a long-standing engagement from which Mrs. Halliday had excused herself at the last minute because of the aforementioned headache. Unless Mrs. Kellerman and a maid were both lying, she had arrived at seven and left at a little before ten.

Rufus Halliday had also dropped in on Victoria Devlin at the Thall house, and then attended a showing of a Navy documentary film at the local theater. Given a small sleepy movie-house like the Fine Arts with its sole lobby attendant, you could get in and out almost at will. And asking the cashier if she had dozed in her cage or left it briefly for a cigarette was like asking a dog if it had been at the roast.

Simon Halliday—Sergeant Tansill stared hard at the next to last name on the list—had taken a client out for cocktails at the Merry-Go-Round Bar, after which he had decided to dine in town before returning home. He had stopped at the Thall house on his way, partly to see if there was any news of Lilac, partly because he had intended to take the Saint Bernard for its evening run.

Charles Storrow, who had been questioned on the slender grounds of having been one of the luncheon group on the day Lilac Thall was drugged—Sergeant Tansill was convinced of that now—said he had spent the evening at home. In a bad way, that boy, the sergeant thought parenthetically. Head over heels about a girl who wasn't having any . . .

And the girl's friend, Victoria Devlin. Tansill lighted a cigarette, dropped the match into his wastebasket and went on looking at her name.

It was a Mrs. Annette Severin who put in the hysterical call to the police at eleven forty-six that morning. She had done up some curtains for Mr. Storrow and had promised to drop them by. Arriving five minutes ago, she had found the front door unlocked and Mr. Storrow himself—more wails began to buffet Sergeant Tansill's ear. He held the instrument a few inches away until the sounds stopped, interrupted another torrent with instructions to stay where she was, put in a call for the coroner and set out, grimly, for Blackfan Road.

Within two hours Charles Storrow's death had taken

on the comfortable shape of suicide. There was the photograph, the relaxed look of peace, the water glass with the dregs which the coroner fingertip-tasted, grimaced at and set aside for analysis.

And there was the crumpled note that had danced itself into the corner of the window between screen and sill. "Lilac: I can't stand" ... Scanty records and memos in the living room desk showed, without need for experts, that it was Storrow's small scrupulous handwriting.

There was the single cocktail glass, washed and dried, on the drainboard in the kitchen, and the opened bottle of sherry beside it.

There was, most convincingly of all, the fact that Charles Storrow had had a bad heart. How bad? W. W. Snaith, M.D., shrugged his shoulders when summoned. "Storrow was—let's see—twenty-eight, I think. He had the heart of a man in his sixties. Oh, he wouldn't have dropped dead for a good many years if he observed the usual precautions. But a dose of sleeping pills that might make the average person sick and stupid would be the finish of him—and obviously was."

W. W. Snaith bowed himself out of the little house and went briskly off on his interrupted calls. The coroner, looking at Sergeant Tansill's brooding expression, said waspishly, "Plain as the nose on your face. Storrow's gone on the Thall girl. She's going to marry somebody else, and meanwhile she's half off her rocker. Storrow can't go on a forgetting binge, he's got to be early to bed and early to rise if he wants to be around for the next census. Maybe under the circumstances he can't stand looking forward to a life of soft-boiled eggs and hot water bottles. Maybe," said the coroner, narrowing shrewd little eyes, "he's overcome with remorse because he tried to kill the Thall girl. He can't have her so nobody else can. 'Each man kills the thing he loves ...' "

Sergeant Tansill used a salty Seacastle term. He added dryly, "I suppose before that he went tearing around after Nurse Corey with a sickle? That took a fair amount of strength and energy, you know. Hardly prescribed exercise for a man in his condition."

"All right," said the coroner, looking abused. "But suicide is what you've got and suicide is what you'll take. I won't be able to tell you when, to a clock-strike—that open window hurried things up a bit. I suppose you'll want that sherry analyzed? Though right about now I could use . . ."

"Funny," said Sergeant Tansill, half to himself, "about that open window, right beside the bed."

"Is it?" The coroner, at the phone, was withering. "The American Medical Journal has just come out with a late bulletin that it's impossible to catch cold after death. . . . Hello, Charley?"

There was going to be snow. The sky was cold and woolly with it, the air had turned brittle, the landscape was sharp and dark and frozen, braced for the first white gusts. At about the time when Mrs. Annette Severin snatched up the phone in the little cottage on Blackfan Road, Victoria Devlin dismissed her cab in front of the Halliday house and knocked on the panelled white door.

The maid let her in. In the fleeting instant before she stepped into the hall Victoria was puzzled by something in the girl's face. What she saw in almost the same startled second over the gray silk shoulder blanked it completely out of her mind.

At the end of the long living room, just visible through the arch of the doorway, Olive Stacey and Rufe Halliday stepped violently out of an embrace. For a moment they were surprised into utter stillness, embarrassment plain on both their faces. Then Rufe had said without pleasure, "It's Victoria," and Olive was moving forward, mechanically assuming the role of hostess. "How nice. You'll stay for lunch, won't you, Victoria? Come inside, there's a fire—isn't it bitter out?"

Shock piled on small shock in Victoria's mind. Olive looked almost pretty. She had washed her hair and it curled faintly on her shoulders; her pointed face was still pink from the blush that had stained it. She was suddenly piquant instead of prim, subtly hazel and gold instead of wren-colored. Or had it been there all the time, a delicate understatement of something close to beauty?

Victoria put speculation aside. "I can't stay, thanks. What I really came for was to talk to you, if you aren't busy."

"Of course." Olive was puzzled but polite. "Come on in—or perhaps we'd better go upstairs."

Her bedroom was small, almost cell-like in its austerity. She said absently, "Sit down, won't you? The bed's quite comfortable. Heavens." She had caught a glimpse of herself in the dressing-table mirror; she sat down abruptly and picked up comb and amber hairpins. Victoria said involuntarily, "Must you? It looks so nice the way it is."

"What . . . oh, this?" Olive touched a long strand of amber-brown hair and beagn to comb it into sleekness, glancing amusedly at Victoria's reflected face. "Well, I'm not a girl of twenty, after all, or so I'm frequently told. And I'm sure the butcher would start over-weighing and the maid would stop dusting behind the furniture if I stopped looking businesslike . . . what did you want to talk to me about, Victoria?"

"Charles Storrow." She hadn't planned exactly how she was going to begin, and it came out with a plunge. "I know that he's dead, although the police don't, yet."

Olive didn't pretend astonishment. Her fingers paused a second in the twisting skein of hair, and then she said slowly, "Oh. I take it you went there, to his house?"

"I was there when you came. When you said you'd found something."

Olive's face in the mirror didn't change. The tilted brook-brown eyes widened a little at Victoria and then slid back to her own reflection. She said, "Oh, were you? What were you doing there, Victoria?"

The casualness of it caught Victoria off guard. "I— wanted to talk to him about something, and I—"

"So did I," said Olive neatly. She thrust a final hairpin into the coil at the nape of her neck and swivelled to face the girl on the bed. "Look here, Victoria. I won't ask you why you hid, nor why you've constituted yourself an inquisitioner. But I will tell you this. I knew Charles Storrow better than the others think—I'd seen him around the village a lot and talked to him often, and I'd always liked him. But it wasn't exactly diplomatic to uphold his cause in this house, where he's considered a young neurotic and a ne'er-do-well—oh, perhaps not by Simon—as well as having the effrontery to aspire to Lilac."

She looked down at her hands, wryly. Victoria waited. Olive said bluntly, "We're all in enough of a mess as it is. Since he'd committed suicide anyway, I thought it would look more—normal if some complete outsider discovered and reported it, as someone undoubtedly will before long. As to the thing I came to tell him about . . ." she glanced

up at Victoria, and for the first time her eyes were wary.
"I—"

There was a gentle tap at the door. In the hall outside
Grace Halliday's serene voice said, "Olive? Janice is asking
about lunch. Should she use what's left of the lamb?"

"The lamb. I'll be right down," Olive called and
turned back to Victoria. But the moment was gone. Remoteness had closed over her face again; in the momentary
withdrawal of her attention she had had time to come to a
decision. She said abruptly, "What I came to tell Charles
Storrow has no bearing on Nurse Corey's death or what
happened to Lilac. I did find something that was better not
made public, and I burned it. And if you tell the police
about it, it's only fair to warn you that I'll deny the whole
thing from start to finish." She stood up and turned away a
little, scooping hairpins into a glass box and straightening
the surface of the dressing table. "Are you sure you won't
stay for lunch? It'll probably be curry."

Victoria had expected shock and confusion; she was
helpless in the face of poise and unconcern and open evasion. She followed Olive down the broad curving staircase,
murmured a greeting to Grace Halliday, felt a far-off surprise at lines and shadows in the older woman's face, and
refused Rufe's offer of a drive back to the East Wind.

The snow had come, weaving and gentle, clung in
fragile white tulle to branches and walls and hedges. Victoria walked towards town in the cold feathery breath of it.
She had learned nothing, except the unexpected sympathy
for Charles Storrow which Olive had freely admitted. And
that Olive had burned the thing she had found. The whole
incident, reported to the police, would sound in the light of
Olive's threatened denial like a desperate and fumbling attempt to implicate someone else.

And Olive and Rufe, moving swiftly out of each
other's arms. Why was that so jarring? They were hardly
related at all, certainly not by any blood tie that counted,
and there could be only a few years between their ages.
Victoria remembered, in view of the illuminating scene she
had witnessed, the way Olive's eyes followed Rufe whenever they were together. Odd that you could be aware of
things without realizing it until they were called forcibly to
your attention ... she had proof of it all over again ten
minutes later.

Her last cigarette had been smoked in Olive's bedroom. Victoria went in to the drug store, bought two packages and glanced idly at a woman at the counter while she waited for change. Glanced and looked away again and then stared.

It hadn't been the maid's expression that had startled her when she was admitted to the Halliday house. It had been the fact of an entirely strange face above the gray silk uniform. The woman sipping a chocolate soda through straws at the end of the counter was the maid who had worked for the Hallidays as late as the dinner on Tuesday night. Before her on the counter, under a pair of worn black cotton gloves, lay Lilac Thall's brown calf handbag.

CHAPTER 15

"I DIDN'T steal anything. I swear I didn't. It seemed too good to be thrown away, and I thought if nobody wanted it . . ."

Esther Schultz looked at Victoria for reassurance and then braced herself under Sergeant Tansill's eye in the Seacastle police station. Fright made her voice rise to a nervous squeak. "It's not as though I was a common thief. I didn't steal it, I never. It was just . . ."

"We know you didn't, Miss Schultz. No one is accusing you of anything, we're only interested in the bag and how you found it. You're absolutely sure," asked Sergeant Tansill, switching his gaze to Victoria, "that this *is* Miss Thall's handbag?"

"I'm positive. It's worn in the same places, and I'd know it anywhere. You can see the pricks down in the right hand corner where her initials were."

Sergeant Tansill peered at miniature holes in the soft leather, nodded, and looked back at the fidgeting maid. "If you'll just tell us, Miss Schultz, when and where you found the bag. . . ."

"Wednesday morning, early," said Esther Schultz. "There's an incinerator around at the back, towards the side of the house. I went out to dump some stuff like I always did first thing in the morning. The pocketbook was buried under a lot of things, but I—" she broke off, scarlet, and tore wretchedly at her gloves.

Sergeant Tansill removed his gaze to the ceiling. "I suppose that like a lot of people the Hallidays sometimes throw away things that are still quite usable even though they're tired of them."

"That's it," said Miss Schultz, damp with mortification and relief. "Gloves, and stockings sometimes with just the start of a run, things like that. But she wouldn't give you yesterday's newspaper, not that one ... well, I saw this pocketbook, and I thought it was an old one of *hers* or maybe Miss Stacey's, and it looked too good to be burnt up and that, and I had nothing to go with my brown so I put it to one side."

"And then?"

"Thursday's my night off. And," said the maid simply, "I was all dressed up in my brown. And just as I was going out the door, with Bob, that's my friend, waiting for me in his car, out comes Mr. Rufe to tell me it's my notice, and they've someone else coming in the morning but they'll pay me for the rest of this week and the next."

She was violently certain that it had not been Rufe who wanted her to go; he had been, she said, embarrassed and upset at having to relay orders from "that one"—Mrs. Halliday. She had gone back to pick up her clothes and other belongings on Friday morning. No, they had never shown any dissatisfaction with her before that, and she had been with them nearly a year. She leaned forward in a sudden pleased burst of confidence.

"That girl they've got now, that Janice Nickerson. I wish them joy of her. She used to work for the Bellocs out on the Point, and she got away with a lace tablecloth and one of a pair of silver candlesticks and ..."

"Now, now, Miss Schultz," said Sergeant Tansill mildly. "Slander ..."

Victoria had sat up in the hard chair near the window. She said, "When you went back on Friday morning, Miss Schultz, did you wear your brown?"

"It was all I had."

"And did you carry the brown bag—this one?"

"Yes."

Victoria caught her breath. She said softly, "And did Mr. Storrow come that morning, while you were there?"

Esther Schultz hesitated. Her eyes went brightly and

alarmedly to Sergeant Tansill. "Didn't someone out there say you'd just gotten back from Mr. Storrow's? He's dead, isn't he?"

"Yes."

"He never," said Miss Schultz staunchly to Victoria.

Ten minutes more shook her. Yes, Charles Storrow had come to the house. Yes, he had gone white as a sheet and asked where she had gotten the bag. But there hadn't been anyone around to hear, and he had left the house before she did.

When the door had closed behind her Sergeant Tansill looked at Victoria with a trace of amusement. "You did very well with her, Miss Devlin."

"We had lunch together."

"Now," said Sergeant Tansill, reaching for the brown calf bag. "There won't be a blasted thing in it, of course, but we'll have a look. . . ."

The hundred to one chance came through. The brown moire lining of the bag was torn. Sergeant Tansill, fishing busily in the slit, brought out a bobby pin, a penny, a stamp and a short newspaper clipping. The clipping said that John Maxwell Gardner, of Chicago, well-known leader in the meat-packing industry, would be at the Waldorf-Astoria in New York for a few days before proceeding to Washington, where he had been appointed chairman of a government advisory committee on meat inspection. With him were Mrs. Gardner and their two young sons, John Maxwell, Jr., and Carmichael. During his stay in New York, Mr. Gardner would address a meeting of . . .

Victoria had stopped listening. Carmichael—after Hope's family, of course. Mrs. John Maxwell Gardner was Hope Carmichael, the Southern belle of Miss Harvey's Academy, who had sworn sweetly and implacably that she would marry well. Victoria was abruptly certain of it because of the linked named and a New York hotel and the fact that Lilac had bothered to tear out and save the clipping.

It might be difficult to get to see the wife of a government committeeman, particularly if you had something to say that she didn't want to hear. Could it have taken five days?

She came back to attention. Sergeant Tansill had summoned a policeman and handed him the clipping, and in the office outside the policeman was asking for long-distance. Across three feet of desk the sergeant was saying musingly, "Tuesday night. You were at the Hallidays' at dinner, I believe, Miss Devlin. You and . . ."

"The Spencers. And Olive Stacey, of course."

"And that was the night you received your call from New York."

"Yes. Have you been able to get in touch with my aunt?"

"No. But I presume you have," said Sergeant Tansill equably, and dismissed it and went on musing. "Tuesday night. The maid found the bag on Wednesday morning, and it looks as though the treasure-hunt was a daily routine with Miss Schultz. I wonder who got rid of Miss Thall's pocketbook in such an amateurish way?"

Tuesday night, black and rainy. Ample cover for a swift trip to the back of the house, a hurried thrusting of the brown bag down among rubbish. And they had all been there when Simon and she arrived at the house—Olive and Grace and Rufe, and Freddy and Millicent Spencer. But why had the purse, which had been in the Thall house as late as Sunday, been kept so long and then clumsily and carelessly disposed of? It must originally have been slated for return, and police surveillance had interfered.

No matter; Charles Storrow had seen and identified the bag, and Charles was dead. Victoria stood. She said, "It proves, doesn't it, that Mr. Storrow didn't commit suicide?"

Sergeant Tansill looked at her under inquiring brows. "Proof? Had you reason to think so before, Miss Devlin?"

That had been stupid. "Of course not."

"Short of a confession, I doubt very much that we'll ever prove it," said the sergeant in a flat hard forgetting voice. "Thanks again, the bag may turn out to be useful. Meanwhile it ought to commend you to Mr. Chesterton."

Victoria turned in the doorway. She had been right then; Chesterton, who was anxious for a quick tidy finish, was the man to fear. Nevertheless, the small jolting shock of it echoed in her voice.

"Does Mr. Chesterton think I attacked Lilac? That I killed Nurse Corey?"

Sergeant Tansill shrugged and took his round gaze away from the snow-curtained window. "Mr. Chesterton thinks you haven't been frank with us, that you've been concealing vital information all along. I'm inclined to agree with him, Miss Devlin."

Victoria hesitated for the seconds it took to smooth on her gloves. But she could hear Chesterton's voice, quiet, clever, gathering itself for the leap. "So you helped Miss Thall set up the mechanics for her own disappearance. You didn't intend that she should ever return alive, did you, Miss Devlin? Was it because she stood between you and Mr. Halliday? And Miss Corey, her devoted childhood nurse, found out about it and threatened to get in touch with her? Was that the way it was, Miss Devlin—or did Mr. Halliday help out when it came to the point of murder and attempted murder? Come now, suppose you let us have your third version—and the truth, this time."

"Thank you, Sergeant," said Victoria in a small cold voice, "I'll be at the East Wind," and went out again into the whitening street.

She was almost at the lane that cut down to Water Street when she caught sight of Esther Schultz again. The Hallidays' former maid had stopped to talk to an acquaintance, and sidewalk traffic was detouring patiently around the two women, a baby in a carriage and a small whimpering child who wanted to go home. On an impulse Victoria paused in front of a bakery window, pretending absorption in a row of cherry pies.

The child carried the day very shortly, its whimpers giving way to a shriek of rage. Esther Schultz's friend bent, gave it a resounding whack, said something cross to the maid and departed with the carriage and the now wailing child.

"Miss Schultz . . . ?"

The woman turned from the curb, her face shuttering as Victoria came forward across the sidewalk. "I don't want anything more to do with the police," she said rapidly. "I told them the truth and there's nothing more to tell. I wish I'd never laid eyes on that bag, but just because . . ."

"It isn't about the bag." The thickly-falling snow had discouraged pedestrians; there was no one within earshot on the windy corner. "Miss Schultz, do you remember a woman in a muskrat coat who came to the house late Thursday morning? She was about forty-five, I'd guess, and wearing a black hat. . . ."

"She came to see Mrs. Halliday," said the maid promptly. "I remember because Mrs. Halliday was lying down upstairs, takes it very easy, that one does, and Olive—Miss Stacey—saw her instead. Reinhardt, her name was."

"Thanks very much," Victoria said. "Oh, by the way, Miss Schultz, I'm afraid I was the cause of your losing your bag. If you think you could get another . . ."

The maid, startled and pleased, pocketed the unobtrusively offered bill. As she was turning away, Victoria said casually, "You have no idea what Miss Reinhardt wanted to see Mrs. Halliday about, I suppose."

"Well . . ." Esther Schultz hesitated. "I'm not sure. But she came to make trouble, that I can tell you. Something about Mr. Simon, by the sound of it, but I guess Miss Stacey calmed her down, because she left in a lot less fuss than she came. . . . You're welcome, I'm sure, Miss, and thank you."

Trouble for Simon, and his family buying it up . . . the woman in the muskrat coat had been pleased as well as vindictive. She had been fired for serious indiscretion, but she had a tale to tell and was being paid not to tell it—and neither Grace Halliday nor Olive Stacey seemed like women who would be frightened easily into submission. But Grace Halliday hadn't seen her after all, and Olive Stacey had "calmed her down."

They should have called Simon, Victoria thought with a feeling of disquiet. Simon would have dealt with her once and for all. . . . On the porch of the East Wind, she brushed snow from her shoulders and the swinging skirts of her coat and went inside and upstairs to her room.

No messages today. She had missed the one that might have saved Charles Storrow's life, because one of the Misses Soames had gotten involved with antimacassars for the parlor chairs, or blueing in the wash or how to stretch the roast. . . .

Victoria watched snow come sheathing down to drown itself in the tossing gray harbor and realized that Charles Storrow's discovery of Lilac's missing handbag hadn't narrowed the circle at all. According to Esther Schultz, there had been no one around when he had noticed and questioned her about it. At any time after that, then, he might have returned—or gone to a phone, dialled a number, made the appointment for his own casual death.

Later in the day, he had visited Bridgewater Hospital. Because a word from Lilac would have told him what he wanted to know?

"He took it like a lamb." Was it enough to bring to the police as proof of murder? Hardly. It was a phrase you used carelessly about a number of things—a broken date, a request for an outrageous favor, bad news of any kind. And yet ... "There's nothing to worry about. He never suspected—"

The other side of the shield, then; the five missing days of Lilac's life, the period about which no one knew anything at all. She had gone to New York, it was almost certain, because Mr. and Mrs. John Maxwell Gardner were to be at the Waldorf-Astoria. And Victoria was stubbornly convinced that Mrs. Gardner was Hope Carmichael—because Lilac's diary for 1941 had been stolen and in 1941 they had all been at Miss Harvey's Academy; because Lilac had cut out and saved the clipping, because she had whispered Hope's name when they lifted her to the stretcher. Most clinchingly of all, because one of the Gardners' sons had been christened Carmichael.

At Miss Harvey's they had paraphrased, "Where there's Hope, there's men." All right, then, Men. Was the frightful thing, the thing Lilac had blurted out long ago to Nurse Corey, concerned with an affair that hadn't been girlish and innocent? Was there a man somewhere who had a hold on Lilac and was employing it after all these years because she was to marry into the Halliday money? A man who had something to do, somehow, with Hope Carmichael Gardner?

Victoria didn't know the exact moment when the small shocking suggestion lifted its head in her mind. It had a horrible air of familiarity, as though it had been waiting a long time to be looked at and examined and accepted.

Blackmail.

She didn't accept it right away. She concentrated fiercely on Miss Harvey's Academy and the possibility of a clue there, and found that her thoughts went wandering back. Nonsense, said Victoria to herself; Lilac would never tolerate blackmail. Nonsense, but just suppose—

Suppose Lilac had tolerated it for eight years, ever since an event which she must have recorded in the stolen diary. Suppose that in desperation, with her marriage to Simon approaching, she had gone to New York for knowledge that would free her—and had found it. "I didn't. I didn't. Hope—"

"Hope says I didn't."

Suppose she had come back to Seacastle to expose her blackmailer—who? Victoria lighted a cigarette and went on thinking, and forgot that Nurse Corey had died because she knew the answer, and Charles Storrow because he had guessed it.

It snowed all that oddly quiet Sunday afternoon, muffling the town in white. Seacastle's excitement had receded now to a pleasurably terrifying glow; people said, marvelling, "When you think that man Fowler might have turned up with the eggs, or the milk!" and "I suppose he couldn't stand the sight of a nurse. Just the white uniform might have set him off, thinking of capture and the asylum again," and "Did you know that the police have been questioning that girl from New York, that friend of Lilac Thall's? She was in the house at the time, apparently, and I had it from Sam Shaw. . . ."

No one knew that a murderous brain was loose and active again.

Towards dark, the temperature rose, the wind shifted, and the snow changed to sleet, lacquering the roads, turning front steps to glass, making shining jeweled shapes of hedges and shrubs and trees. In the meantime, three telephone calls had reached Victoria Devlin at the East Wind.

The first was from a student nurse at Bridgewater Hospital.

"Miss Devlin? I shouldn't be doing this, but Miss Thall has been so nice and she asked me as a favor if I'd call when I got off."

"Yes?"

"She's only allowed one visitor in the evening, you know, and then only for a few minutes. There's someone supposed to be coming at eight, but if you'd come at a little before that, maybe at quarter of, they wouldn't be able to get in. Miss Thall says she doesn't want to hurt any feelings, but she'd rather see you."

"Oh. You don't know who—?"

"No." The voice grew prim and a little frightened. "You understand I'm not supposed to be doing this at all. I don't know what they'd say at the hospital. But Miss Thall's been awfully pleasant to me and I can't see any harm. . . ."

"Of course not. Thanks very much," said Victoria,

queerly conscious of suspense. "If you're back on duty again and you see her, will you tell her I'll be there?"

The second telephone call was from Simon Halliday; the turmoil at the agency over the lost account and the firing of Miss Reinhardt had sent him in when he would ordinarily have been home. He said without prelude, "Will you have dinner with me tonight, Victoria?"

"No."

"Oh—are you busy?"

"Well, I . . ." Telephone silence, the loudest lack of sound in the world, hung for a moment. Victoria thought racingly, avoiding him entirely is worse, it's as much as saying I don't trust myself with him. And maybe he knows something about the calf bag. . . .

"I'm not, actually. But it would have to be early."

"Six all right? I'll pick you up. Better alert the Miss Soameses, they won't want to be scooped by the egg man."

Miss Agatha Soames, the errand-runner for the trio by virtue of being the youngest, was indignant when she mounted the stairs for the third time. If Miss Devlin were content like anybody else to look at a magazine in the parlor, there wouldn't be any need for dashing up and down these flights as though she were twenty again. She tapped, said coldly, "Telephone, Miss Devlin. MY, but you're a busy young lady," and trotted breathlessly down the stairs again to hover in the parlor.

The phone call was from Sergeant Tansill. He said, "Seeing as how you found the brown bag, Miss Devlin, I thought you'd be interested in how the lead on the newspaper clipping came out. We didn't find the Gardners at the Waldorf-Astoria or any other New York hotel."

"Oh." It was a thudding disappointment; she'd spent her afternoon building on that.

"Apparently J. M. Gardner is very touch-me-not since he's gotten himself named to a government committee, and went to ground in some hotel or apartment where even reporters couldn't find him. But," said Sergeant Tansill expressionlessly, "they're back at Lockwood Avenue, Tower Hills, Chicago, and we were able to reach them there. And neither of them ever heard of Lilac Thall."

CHAPTER 16

WHEN you come to the end of a perfect theory—somehow it wouldn't turn into music. Victoria thanked Sergeant Tansill for letting her know and went slowly back upstairs, to her room, thinking a number of bitter things.

It served her right for supposing she could out-reason the police. It whittled her neatly and cruelly down to size—an over-confident amateur far out of her depth in a situation which could be handled only by trained minds and experienced men.

Victoria drowned the rest of it out in the shower; it was a quarter of six and Simon would be arriving. In her new state of emptiness and shock she dressed and fastened hoops of jet in her ears and paused before the wavy mirror, remembering the night Jim Patterson had given her these earrings. "Black," he'd said, laughing, "for my only blonde. Though you aren't blonde really, come to think of it, which I frequently do. Ash, rather. But don't imagine I'm in love with you, just because I carry your picture around in my wallet and go mooning about after earrings and cut myself shaving and send a check for the laundry to my parents in California and a letter to Whitestone beginning, 'Dear Mother and Dad' . . ."

Her hair fell in a soft pale sweep beside Jim Patterson's earrings. Victoria turned away from the mirror, heard the front door open and Simon Halliday's voice say,

"Thanks, but I'm waiting for Miss Devlin," and caught up her coat and gloves.

"I've heard," said Simon carefully, "about Charles Storrow. It was pretty plain how he felt about Lilac, poor guy, but none of us thought—"

"It wasn't suicide." Victoria's voice was fierce and bitter; it brought his eyes intently up to hers. "I know it wasn't. If he'd been going to kill himself he'd have done it when everyone thought Lilac was dead—you must see that. Someone killed him, Simon, because he found out who struck Lilac and killed Nurse Corey. It must have been the person who stole Lilac's handbag, because—"

"I've missed the beginning," Simon said, giving her a bright, worrying look, "so suppose you start from there. What about the bag?"

He was silent when she finished, moving a salt cellar about in long competent fingers, upending it to make a little white hill on the tablecloth. "And Olive said she'd burned whatever it was she found?"

"Yes. It must have been the engagement book, or," said Victoria, "the diary. The same name must have occurred in both of them, if both of them had to be stolen. But that lead's gone up in smoke now."

"Lilac will get her memory back." Simon made a star out of the salt, drawing it in long powdery points. "They say there's no permanent damage to the brain itself. She'll remember where she was and why she came back to Seacastle as she did in those widow's clothes. Chances are that'll lead to the rest of it."

The soup arrived. Victoria stirred hers and said suddenly, "But do you realize that if she remembers she may be in more danger than ever? Someone tried to kill her, after all, someone . . ."

"She's in the hospital now. The police aren't allowed to badger her, but don't think they don't know what's going on. No one would dare lay a finger on her when she's more or less under guard."

But I'm being allowed to see her, thought Victoria, and if I, why not someone else, just as surreptitiously? The susceptible student nurse might have made another phone call, might have said to another voice, "I'd rather you didn't tell anyone. . . ." It was a chilling thought. She asked Simon if he had been aware of an attachment between

Rufe and Olive Stacey, and was rewarded with a look of astonishment.

"Are you sure? Good Lord—I suppose it was inevitable in a way. But Rufe would have told me if there'd been anything settled—at least," said Simon bitterly, "he would have told me before all this happened. We've all changed, we've all got something to hide. Even you, Victoria. You've changed more than any of us."

Victoria didn't answer. She sat very still while the waiter removed the soup plates and brought steak, and heard Simon saying gently, "You know it's been different, don't you?"

Victoria laced tight fingers under the edge of the tablecloth. How dismaying the truth would be if you came out from behind the diplomatic code, if you broke faith with the trusting way in which people asked dangerously leading questions. "Yes, it's been different because I've fallen in love with you, and the thought of your marrying Lilac is insupportable. May I have the salt, please?"

Incredibly, she hadn't spoken aloud; Simon was still looking at her curiously. Victoria said, "Different? It could hardly help being, could it? Things haven't been exactly routine for any of us during the past week, and Lilac's still far from well. In fact, things may be even more different by tomorrow, if Mr. Chesterton has his way and I take up residence in jail."

Simon stared. "You mean there's been actual talk of an arrest? Why didn't you let me know? I'll see Somers—he's in the commissioner's office, used to be a friend of my father's. . . . What have they dreamed up by way of a motive, or have they come to that yet?"

"Oh, we're madly in love, didn't you know?" She could be cool now and a little amused. "Or so I gather from the trend of Mr. Chesterton's questions. But don't worry, Simon—I was the instigating villain. Have you ever heard anything so—"

But Simon had moved violently, so that a fork went clattering to the floor. He stared at her a moment longer, his face full of shock, before he put a hand over his eyes and said gently and hopelessly, "Oh, God."

Victoria's heart gave one tremendous lurch and steadied again as she gazed in dismay at flowers on another table. What had she done? In reaching for poise and balance, she had smashed to pieces the delicate and fragile pretense between herself and the man across the table. She wasn't alone in the thing that was so dreadful a betrayal of Lilac. Simon felt it too: the sudden sweep of emotion that wiped out past relationships and made future ones meaningless, that temporarily sponged away other loyalties and older obligations. But not for long. Her brief dazed feeling of exultation was gone before it had matured; she was glancing at a gilt-framed clock high on a distant wall and saying with forced matter-of-factness, "Would you mind if we didn't have coffee? It's getting late. . . ."

And Simon, who might never have given her that one wild lost look, was answering, "Of course. . . . Check, please."

They were Lilac's best friend and Lilac's fiancé again, going briskly out into the icy sleeting night.

The roads were polished black glass, the windshield frozen and opaque. Even if she called a cab as soon as she got back to the East Wind she couldn't be at the hospital before eight with dangerous driving conditions like these. But Lilac's scheduled visitor might be delayed too, and there was still a good chance that she could arrive there first. Tension began its slow build; she *must* get there first.

More to bridge the dark stiff silence in the car than anything else, Victoria said, remembering, "Oh, Simon. Miss Reinhardt, from your office . . ."

"Miss Reinhardt?" Simon's hands jerked on the wheel; the car slewed, made a lazy arc on ice. Simon turned with the skid, maneuvered cautiously back onto his own side of the road and said more gently, "What do you know about Miss Reinhardt?"

Victoria was bewildered and a little angry at the almost savage way in which he had echoed the name. She said crisply, "I don't know anything about her except what your maid—the woman who used to be your maid, rather—told me. That she came the other day to make trouble, and—"

"When?"

He hadn't been told; Victoria felt confused and out of her depth. "Thursday—the day I went back to New York."

Simon listened to the few bare facts in silence. When she had finished he said softly, "Well, now. I wonder . . ." and left it there.

They were on Water Street, going past the ranks of weathered old houses, the boatyard with its bony thrusting spars, the faint waxy splashing of streetlamps. Victoria glanced at Simon's frowning profile and gathered her courage. "Why was she let go—the maid?"

"Why—? Oh." Simon brought his mind back with an obvious effort. "Rufe missed money from his wallet a couple of times, and there was a cigarette box and a couple of other things that suddenly weren't around any more—why?"

"I wondered, that's all." Lies, Victoria thought detachedly. Who had spun them to get rid of the woman with her potentially dangerous knowledge? They were at the East Wind. She said, "Thanks very much, Simon. It was a wonderful dinner."

Simon opened the porch door. He said constrainedly, "You'll let me know, won't you, if there's any more talk of their arresting you tomorrow? You'll get in touch with me right away?"

"Of course, but I hope I won't need to. Good-night."

When the front door had closed behind him Victoria picked up the hall telephone. The first two taxi companies refused the drive to Bridgewater Hospital over the icy roads; the third said warily that it would cost her something and they could have a car there within fifteen minutes.

Fifteen minutes—there was still a chance. Victoria went up the narrow tan-carpeted stairs to her room. You didn't lock your door at the East Wind, you never even had a key. It might have been the subconscious awareness of that fact that made her step back sharply as she opened the door on darkness.

Had there been movement inside the room, or was it only the sound of a drawn breath that was not her own? Victoria waited, one hand gripping the door frame and the other clenched stiffly at her side, and all at once the light sprang on inside the room.

"Millicent! Why on earth—?" Her nerves had tricked her; she had thought for a moment that there was danger on the other side of that half-opened door. Victoria closed it behind her and watched Millicent Spencer's eyes narrow and then widen again as they grew accustomed to the light. Freddy's wife had been restless while she waited; she was smoking one of her rare cigarettes. While Victoria closed the door she put the glass ashtray down on the bedside table and crushed the end of the cigarette in it. "Freddy doesn't know I'm here," she said a little breathlessly, "and the three old women who run this place are the worst gossips in Seacastle. I thought if I just waited . . ."

Just waited—silently, in the dark? There was something delicately wrong with that, something more than the surface oddness. Victoria sat down on the bed without taking off her coat and said, "Did you want to talk to me, Millicent?"

"Yes, I—I've got to." Millicent was frightened and hostile at the same time; she darted a quick look at Victoria, gaugingly, before she sat down on the edge of the little rocker at the window. "You heard us talking last night at the Cabot House, Freddy and me, didn't you?"

"At dinner? Now that you mention it . . . yes, I did." Victoria kept excitement out of her voice. Go on tiptoe here, they didn't know how much she'd heard.

"Well, I can't stand it," Millicent said unsteadily. "Whispering and sneaking and being afraid that . . . I just can't stand it any more, that's all. I told Freddy he should have got out of it long ago, I told him you were suspicious and you wouldn't be the only one." Her mouth was trembling, her small well-groomed hands tore at each other in her lap. "And now there's that woman. . . ."

That woman . . . Miss Reinhardt? Victoria, sitting dazed and uncomprehending on the bed, hid her bewilderment. Millicent would retreat in her pink stubborn way if she had the slightest suspicion that she could come out of this without confessing all of what she assumed was partly known.

Was it too late already? Millicent had sat up straighter in the rocking chair, her measuring blue gaze was turning shrewd. Victoria flicked a speck of dust from her coat and said boldly, at random, "I suppose you're talking about Simon's former secretary?"

At that, Millicent's tentative groping for composure ended completely. The knowledge that had been tormenting her began to spill out in a gasping flood, and Victoria listened and lighted a cigarette and tried to conceal astonishment and disgust.

It hadn't been Flora Reinhardt who had passed on campaign plans to another advertising agency, for which the hitherto mysterious Mr. Fox was an account executive. It had been Freddy Spencer, who had several times received plump and encouraging bonuses from Fox.

"Layouts," said Millicent, calming in the face of utter disaster, "and headlines and copy themes—everything. This other agency does a lot of trade advertising for other accounts in the same general field. Biscuits, it was the first time, and then plated silver. So that clients who got interested in the stuff Simon's agency worked out for them would see the same thing by a competitor a week or two later in one of the trade papers. It acted two ways, you see. . . ."

Yes, thought Victoria with loathing, it would. Besides providing a rich natural resource for Mr. Fox's agency, the material that Freddy Spencer removed would convince prospective clients that Simon's agency was boldly plagiarizing. Halliday, Pierce and Brittain dealt mainly in national advertising, and months had to elapse between the inception of a campaign and its ultimate appearance. While retail and trade ads could be whipped together in a matter of days and weeks. . . . Victoria felt sick, remembering Freddy's affable, innocent face and genial hum. She said, "I suppose Freddy lost Miss Reinhardt her job?"

Millicent looked evasively away. "She'll get another job. He had to do it, because the directors were demanding an investigation."

"Oh, I see—he might have lost his own job."

"That's it," Millicent said eagerly, rising above irony. "That's why he had to make it look as though she'd been responsible—she used to work there with Simon, you know, at the other agency." Millicent drew a long shaky breath, flushed at Victoria's silence and said with sudden venom, "Oh, I know what you're thinking. But we're not the only ones. Ask Simon's dear, sweet aunt where she gets the money for imported British tweeds and a sable cape and a houseful of cut flowers. Ask her where . . ." Her voice tumbled on, vicious, out of control.

Victoria turned away with a feeling of uncleanness. She said levelly, "I suppose her husband . . ."

"Her husband didn't leave her a cent. A cousin of Freddy's works in the law office that handles the Halliday estate, and he knows. It's all coming out of Simon and Rufe's pockets," said Millicent triumphantly. "Oh, there'll be an accounting one of these days—when Simon marries. Then they'll see how far she's to be trusted."

Lines and shadows, an abrupt look of age in Grace Halliday's charming face, her barely-sensed relief that Simon wasn't to be married immediately after all—it might be true. Whether it was or not, it was a matter that concerned only Simon and Rufe and their aunt. Victoria turned and looked curiously at Millicent.

"When this thing at the agency first became noticeable, Freddy wanted to go to Lilac, didn't he?"

"Yes." As suddenly as she had flared into rage, Millicent sagged again. She didn't meet Victoria's eyes. "He thought she might—help in some way, get Simon to cover up for Freddy somehow until the worst of it blew over and he could get in the clear again."

"But you didn't think she would, did you?" Victoria forgot the passing of time and the cab that would be arriving at any minute, was only dimly aware of the strangeness of being shut away with Lilac's sister, hearing confidences brought out in a small alien bedroom. "Why do you hate her so, Millicent?"

Sleet hit the window and bounced microscopically on the sill. Millicent stood up, her back to Victoria, and rubbed a clear spot on the blurred black pane. She said calmly, "What a frightful night. . . . You usually hear, don't you, Victoria, about older sisters who have everything? And the younger ones that are left out in the cold and get fobbed off with the second best of whatever it is? Well, it was the other way around in our house."

Victoria made an involuntary sound. Millicent said without turning, "Oh, yes, I was the good girl. I was the one they showed off to the aunts in Pittsburgh, I was the one who never got her dresses torn or her hair full of burrs or an F in conduct. I thought," said Millicent, facing Victoria at last, "that that was what made people like you."

It was indecent, it was pitiful, it was the sort of thing you ought never to hear. Victoria murmured and rose, but Millicent looked fixedly at her and said, "I thought you wanted to hear this, Victoria. . . . Anyway, that isn't what people like. Lilac had—has—whatever it is, charm, or amusingness— I don't know what you'd call it. She's always had men, and I—" Millicent broke off fumblingly, and Victoria knew that she was thinking of her husband, Freddy, of his sandy head that came to a point in back and his soft plump hands, of his anxious eyes and his furtive negotiations with Mr. Fox. And of Charles Storrow, who had at least been honest and young and sincere, and Simon, who was everything Freddy wasn't.

"But I didn't," continued Millicent, still staring at Victoria, "give Lilac anything—any kind of drug—that day she ran her car into the hedge, if that's what you're thinking." Her face flushed, not its usual placid pretty pink but an angry bitter scarlet. "Oh, I don't expect you to believe me. Freddy doesn't, I know, I saw how nervous he got when you started asking about the lunch that day. But just because I—" She broke off abruptly, her eyes flickering away.

"Because you took Lilac's car last Sunday, and pretended to be Lilac, Freddy thought you'd been responsible for the drugs too." Victoria said it softly, not wanting to snap the thread.

"Yes. But after all," Millicent said, eyes bright and defiant again, "Lilac *wasn't* in Seacastle over the weekend, even though you won't admit it, and she wasn't sick. She's got the constitution of an ox, in the first place—and you can't tell me Nurse Corey would have gone all the way to the third floor with trays and things even if she had been ill. No, Lilac was giving us all a runaround for reasons of her own, and I thought if she heard rumors that she'd been seen out driving she'd be forced into coming back, and," said Millicent with startling viciousness, "that she'd land in trouble with her precious Hallidays."

This was the one thing, Victoria thought, sitting silent and expressionless on the bed, that Lilac hadn't counted on. She had known better than to trust her sister, but she hadn't realized how cruelly sharp the eyes of hatred could be.

Millicent was making small gathering motions, as though she were ready to leave. She said flatly, "You're Lilac's friend, but you don't know her. How strong she can be, or how—brutal, or how sure she is that she'll always have the luck she's had all her life. Maybe she will. But maybe . . . do you see my gloves anywhere, Victoria?"

The gloves were on the floor behind the night table. Victoria retrieved them, not looking at Millicent's still-naked face. "I'm sorry, Millicent. I had no idea. . . ."

"Oh well," said Millicent conclusively, and was almost herself again, pink and firm and ready to raise an eyebrow at anything outside her own small sphere. She halted at the door. "You won't tell anyone about Freddy, about what I've told you?"

"No," said Victoria, because anything else was impossible, and closed the door behind her. She hadn't asked Millicent about Lilac's pink and gold kerchief but she was almost certain, in the light of what she had just heard, what had happened. After using Lilac's convertible and carefully re-taping the key into place, Millicent had forgotten that she still wore the kerchief and had stuffed it into her bag. Later, when the alarm went out for Lilac, she had been afraid to dispose of it completely; it was needed to bolster up the illusion that Lilac had been out in her car. She couldn't risk another trip to the Thall garage, and so she had had Freddy toss it somewhere near the spot where the dead nurse had lain.

Mechanically, Victoria used lipstick and a comb. The oilskinned figure she had seen hurrying down to the harbor had been, of course, Millicent's thoroughly panicked husband. Chance and the wind had blown the kerchief into the water and under the pier. Whereupon the police, instead of reconstructing an appointment between Lilac and the nurse, had assumed that Lilac too had been killed and her body flung into the water. That accounted for Millicent's near-hysteria later on, when she saw the grim official machinery that her ruse had set in motion. . . .

A horn sounded distantly in the street. A moment after that a man's voice in the hall shouted, "Taxi?"

"Coming," Victoria called, and dropped her compact into her bag and went to the bedside table to turn out the lamp. As the room slipped into darkness her coat sleeve caught the glass ashtray, and she closed the door on the thunderous sound of it hurtling under the bed.

It wasn't until she was settled in the back of the cab, watching crystal and jet glitter past the windows, that Victoria began to wonder about the strange little interview with Millicent Spencer. Freddy didn't know his wife had come—or had he sent her there with the distressingly frank tale that called for pity and contempt more than anything else?

Because she had realized what it was that had bothered her earlier. A link formed and strengthened between the indefinable air of movement in the darkness as she started to enter her room and the echoing crash, later, of the ashtray that Millicent had replaced on the night table. It wasn't pleasant to think that Lilac's sister had waited behind the door in blackness, with that heavy shining square of glass in her hands.

CHAPTER 17

THE clock in the hospital lobby said eighteen minutes after eight. It wasn't a time to risk refusal at the desk, where a nurse was hunting through a card file and saying querulously, "How do you spell it?" to a spectacled man in a brown coat. Victoria walked boldly past, fell into step with two women brandishing visiting cards, and reached the safety of the elevator.

If only she wasn't too late, if only Lilac's other visitor had been delayed similarly by ice and sleet and circumstance. . . . At the third-floor desk the nurse said severely, recognizing her, "You're the young lady who stayed too long with Miss Thall yesterday, aren't you? I'll call Dr. Lemon and find out if she's allowed a visitor this evening. . . ."

She said, "Yes, doctor," interminably into the telephone while Victoria waited, gripping her pocketbook with tight nervous fingers. At least there wasn't anyone with Lilac, she had gotten here first after all. The nurse said a final, "Yes, doctor," and hung up. "No more than fifteen minutes, Miss Devlin. You know your way, don't you? . . ."

Lilac's room, heavy with the fragrance of massed roses on the bureau, was in hushed dark-gold shadow. Lilac was propped up a little in the white bed, a magazine unopened beside her, the flat outline of her body under the coverlet giving her the curiously feeble and vulnerable look

of all people immobilized among medicines and cunning
steel instruments on trays and the faint occasional scent of
ether. She moved her head a fraction as the door opened,
and said through pale lips, "Oh, Victoria. Thank you for
coming, I hoped you'd be able . . . they'll let you stay a
little while, won't they?"

"Fifteen minutes." Better to let her know, so that she
would say what she had made up her mind to say without
sparring and halting and deciding against it completely.
"How do you feel, Lilac?"

"Better, thanks. I wish you'd sit down, Victoria. You
look so impermanent."

She knows. She remembers, thought Victoria without
conscious surprise. Because an awareness of something
that disturbed and frightened Lilac was there in the narrow white face, in the grayness under restless eyes, the
constant small motions of the long-fingered hands. Lilac's
ring finger, Victoria noticed for the first time, was bare.
Perhaps they had made her remove Simon's diamond, and
he or Millicent had taken it home for safe-keeping.

Lilac had followed her glance. She said, "It's too bad,
isn't it? I've told Simon how sorry I am about it's being
stolen. Perhaps the police will be able to get it back." She
was lying—badly, almost indifferently. Victoria stared at
her a moment and then looked sharply away.

So that was to be it—a trumped-up tale of attack by a
tramp, a casual thief, with no more motive than a chance
glimpse of the platinum-mounted diamond. Victoria was
suddenly angry at the girl stretched so coolly in the hospital bed. Lilac had started all this with her mysterious trip
to New York, had been the cause of two deaths, could,
with the knowledge locked behind her stubborn secret face,
release all her friends—all but one—from the morass of
fear and suspicion and violence into which her own actions
had plunged them. Victoria said crisply, "There isn't too
much time, Lilac. Was there something you wanted me to
do for you?"

"Yes," said Lilac, and hesitated and drew a long
breath. "Have you anything that would do for paper, and a
pencil? If you could deliver a note for me . . ."

She wrote rapidly on the back of a laundry list Victoria handed her, folded the slip of paper and slid it into a
florist's envelope that had come with the roses. She sealed
it without meeting Victoria's eyes. She said, sending shock

through Victoria like a small boiling wave of nausea, "Do you think you could manage to get that to Charles Storrow?"

Sleet hurled itself against the window in a silence that was all at once macabre. It shouldn't have been so jolting. They hadn't told her, of course; invalids in Lilac's condition subsisted on custards and fruit juices and trivial good news. Victoria turned her back on Lilac and went to the bureau for her bag and gloves, and looked in the flower-banked mirror at soft red roses and ferns and her own blank face, edged with gold from the light behind her. She heard her voice saying, "I'll try," as she dropped the little envelope into her purse, and then, "I'd better go, Lilac, I'm in disrepute with the nurse as it is. Is there anything you'd like anyone to bring you? Good-night, then. I'm glad you're so much better...."

In the outer lobby near the doors, unconscious of the gusts of cold air let in by arriving and departing visitors, Victoria opened the florist's envelope and unfolded the note that Lilac had written to a dead man. She read it twice before she tore it into snowflake pieces and poked them deep into sand in a cigarette receptacle in the corner.

Her cab was waiting; the driver remarked sourly that he had been forced to move twice and he thought he had lost her and the company ought to have known better than to send any of its cars out on a night like this. And Victoria, blind and deaf and in the grip of an almost unbearable excitement, said only, "I think there's a drug store at the bottom of the hill. Would you mind stopping there a minute?"

In the drug store, at a counter piled with lavender hot water bottles and makeup kits for invalids, she bought a flashlight and ran back across the slippery sidewalk. She waited until they reached Seacastle and had turned into Water Street before she said, "You can let me off here, driver," and, a moment later, turned and began to walk into sleety cloaking darkness.

The secrecy, the lonely rattling night around her, were essential to the plan that Lilac had had in mind for Charles Storrow. Because she had been very anxious that no one should know of this eleventh-hour trip to the Thall garage.

Sergeant Tansill pushed aside the coroner's report on Charles Storrow, yawned, looked longingly at his watch and picked up another typewritten sheet. The alienist's findings after a second interview with Lilac Thall at Bridgewater Hospital were discouragingly lengthy and cumbersome. It reminded Sergeant Tansill of the way valuable ornaments were packed—excelsior and corrugated board and wadded newspaper and more excelsior and somewhere at the heart of it all the tiny precious thing itself.

"In this interviewer's opinion . . ." It went fatly, polysyllabically on; the Thall case was obviously a joy to the alienist's soul. Towards the end, a phrase leaped out of the incomprehensible wordage; ". . . memory almost if not completely restored, with fear motive, possibly sub-conscious, fighting confession impulse. Subject markedly uncooperative . . ."

The alienist had broken down, at the end. A pencilled scrawl running around the margin said, "You can't get blood out of a stone. Medically speaking the girl isn't up to cross-examination, won't be for days. Give her enough rope and chances are she'll hang somebody."

Enough rope . . . Sergeant Tansill stared bitterly at the report. Patrolmen Peters put a mournful face around the door and looked pointedly at his watch. "We going to stay here all night?"

"Maybe," said Sergeant Tansill, unmoved.

It was then that the phone rang. It was the third-floor superintendent at the hospital, flurried a little out of her usual preciseness. "Sergeant Tansill? You wanted to know about any visitors Miss Thall had this evening. There was only one. Miss Devlin arrived at eight-twenty and left at eight-thirty-two."

Sergeant Tansill listened and scowled at his desk-top and said in a baffled voice, "That's all—you're sure of it? Nobody else might have asked for Miss Thall at the downstairs desk without your knowing it, or slipped by . . . ?"

"I assure you," said the nurse, bridling invisibly, "that we have been most careful, Sergeant. We are accustomed to looking after human lives twenty-four hours a day, you know, and I have never left my desk for one moment since seven-thirty, when visiting hours began. Let me emphasize again, Sergeant . . ."

Sergeant Tansill sighed and eventually hung up; scratched aimlessly on his blotting pad, said musingly to it, "Now, how do you like that?" and looked at it some more.

Then he picked up the phone abruptly and dialled a number.

It was one of the shortest phone calls Patrolman Peters had ever heard him make. In the course of it Sergeant Tansill said, "You're sure? . . . Better check . . . Thanks."

Seconds later, the sergeant was only the echo of a shouted order at Patrolman Peters, the banging of the door and the racing, swivelling departure of a police car into the freezing dark.

The garage door handle was coated with ice; the door itself slid back only after repeated shouldering thrusts. Inside, there was the distantly familiar smell of oil and gasoline and damp cement. Victoria closed the door behind her and felt her way into thick blackness, moving past Lilac's car to the darkroom door.

The enlarger and the printing frame—that was where Lilac had instructed Charles Storrow to look. Victoria groped for the knob of the darkroom door and pulled it to behind her, her nerves flinching from the frightening, horror-story sound of creaking unused hinges. Only then did she dare take the flashlight from her bag and switch it on to bring the narrow little room dancing up out of darkness.

The one high window had been boarded shut. To her right was a table against the wall, stained with chemicals, holding only a pile of enamel trays and a metal washer with some forgotten negatives hooked in dry, cobwebbed emptiness. At the end of the darkroom were two small set tubs with rusted faucets; at her left the old-fashioned enlarger, long and black and hooded eerily in cloth, rested on another home-made table. A printing frame was still in place at the end of the table. Victoria moved over to it and began to unfasten the clasps at the back of the frame.

Incredible, said her galloping mind, that there should have been something hidden here that the police hadn't bothered to make a thorough search for. But they had apparently assumed what she and Simon and the others had—that Lilac's attacker had bundled her body in here for purposes of concealment after striking her outside in the driveway. But Lilac had been followed here when she came to cache her precious find, and had moved quickly and expertly in familiar darkness. And then she had been warned, perhaps by some tiny sound, and had drawn breath for a scream she wasn't allowed to utter. There wouldn't have been time then for her assailant to have made a complete search, because he or she had had to know beforehand that Lilac was expected at eight and that an investigation might begin at once. . . .

The clasps were open. The streaked and yellowed piece of what had once been glossy printing paper fell away from green plush backing. And there was something else—a creased snapshot with bent corners. This was what Charles Storrow had been sent to get.

Victoria picked it up and stared in bewilderment at what was evidently a night fire scene in an ugly frame house. A blur in the foreground wore a fireman's hat, a woman in a bathrobe on the steps of the house clutched a small shaggy-headed child. On the porch, in shadow, a man and a woman had their faces partially averted. Both wore night clothes—the man pajamas and a suit coat, the woman a nightgown under a bathrobe. Victoria held the snapshot closer and felt her heart give one heavy shocked thud as familiarity leaped out of the utterly foreign setting.

She stood completely still for a moment, examining, memorizing. The other face was distinctive but strange, couldn't possibly have been anyone here in Seacastle unless the camera had distorted it beyond recognition. Still dazed, suspended in unreality, Victoria dropped the snapshot into her handbag and turned to the enlarger.

How did you get inside? After moments of helpless fumbling she threw back the cloth, unscrewed the lens and its attachment and thrust a narrowed hand inside. Almost immediately her fingers closed on something slippery and soft and cool. It was an evening bag of striped silk, curiously heavy in spite of its small and fragile appearance. Victoria drew it all the way out through the mouth of the enlarger, and in almost the same instant took a swift step and clicked off the flashlight, blotting the room into darkness.

It had probably been the wind, shuddering around the garage door, that had made that brief low rumble of sound. The wind, or the vibration of fear on her own strung nerves . . . get out of here, at once. This was, she realized for the first time, a cul-de-sac, a small musty trap from which there was no retreat but the door to the garage. Still holding the evening bag, she picked up the flashlight and started gently forward. The hinge of the darkroom door creaked drawlingly as she turned the knob and pushed.

"Victoria?"

It was no more than a whisper, a feathery brush of sound; it was far more terrifying than a thunderclap. It was the delicate tentacled approach of danger, made more frightful by the softness of the summons. "Victoria?"

She shrank against the long work-table, wood biting at the small of her back, holding her breath until it was a bursting pain in her lungs and then releasing it, torturedly, a little at a time.

"I won't hurt you, Victoria dear," said the whisper. "I only want to talk to you. Come out, won't you?"

In the garage, near the outside doors, a flashlight flared briefly, was muffled to dull copper by cupping fingers. From where she stood Victoria could look slantingly out at a fold of brown topcoat, a reaching arm, an open toolchest with a heavy wrench sprawled on top. The flashlight went out. There was a furtive click of disturbed metal.

The wrench.

"Victoria? You're in there, aren't you?" Cautiously, the tiptoed march began. Victoria edged silently back, feeling with her hands to prevent a tell-tale collision with the enlarging table, until she had reached the tubs at the back of the darkroom and there was no further retreat. To die like this, under the vicious swing of a wrench; to become in a few short hours a dissection exercise for the coroner, the investigation into the death of Victoria Devlin; to be stretched and manipulated and touched judiciously with becoming makeup by an undertaker . . . Horrifyingly, Victoria's throat began to convulse with aching tears.

This was purely physical fear, the dread of bone being crushed, the wincing of flesh from the killing blow. The footsteps were closer now but the whisper remained the same, the sexless lift into audibility that might have been a man's voice, womanishly raised, or a woman's voice lowered into an ugly attempt at reassurance.

"I know you're right here, Victoria. I'll find you." Benign, like a spinster muttering absently to a missing spool of thread. There was a hideously intimate quality to the search, a wheedling, confiding air. "You know who I am, don't you, so you know that I'd never harm you. You've only to turn on your flashlight—you must have one—and see."

But she didn't know. She couldn't be sure. . . .

Victoria dropped down on her hands and knees and crushed herself under the tubs. 'You've only to turn on your flashlight'—but the searcher had one, so why this slow fumbling approach in the dark when the eye of the flashlight would find her instantly?

She realized then, slowly and laboriously, the significance of the heavy little evening bag she was still gripping in one hand.

There was a weapon of some sort in it. Her searcher was afraid of becoming a target.

A gun.

She had never held a gun in her hand before, didn't know how to tell when it was ready to fire. But this was something, this was a small frail threat of her own. There was a blundering sound as the advancing figure bumped against the enlarging table; under cover of it Victoria had snapped open the silk evening bag and was groping for what seemed like a logical hold on cold unfamiliarly-shaped metal.

"I'm sure we've come for the same thing," said the whisper coaxingly. Close, now, shockingly close; a kneeling swing would find her. "It ought to be turned over to the police, you know. You've only to toss it out on the floor, Victoria, and I'll take it and go."

Pause. And the slow, silent mount of rage. "All right, then. You're under here, aren't you?" Metal crashed violently against wood at the enlarging table. Victoria put a hand bruisingly over her mouth to lock in screams of hysteria as the wrench slashed down deafeningly again. The whisper was panting now, with exertion and pent-up fury. "You're a fool, you know, going through all this. Or did you know that your dear friend Lilac was a murderess? No better than William Fowler, no better than an animal? . . . I'll give you one more chance, Victoria, and then I'm going to turn on the light and you're going to hand over what you've found—"

Victoria tightened her fingers around the gun. Could you hit anything if you didn't know how to shoot? Did you hold the thing steady at your waist, and then press? No, that was a camera. Camera . . . Snapshot . . . she couldn't, she mustn't go out of control now. Cautiously, hardly breathing, she inched herself out from under the cold metal roof of the tubs and stood erect. And the flashlight sprang on, a roar of sequins in blackness, and she pulled desperately on the tiny curve of steel against the inside of her finger.

There was the dynamiting sound of the shot, and she had missed. The flashlight toppled, and the voice in mad gold-angled darkness came out from behind its silky whispering mask and said with savage venom, "I'll ... show ... you ..."

She knew the voice now. She had only time to think desperately, Simon, *Simon*, before the onrush of splitting, ploughing pain.

CHAPTER 18

". . . get off, is there?"

"Not a chance in the world."

Victoria's head ached swollenly, her eyelids were made of iron. If she lay very still the voices would go away. It wasn't dawn yet, and they had no right to wake her; one wavering glimpse had shown her the darkness at the window before she closed her eyes again. But there was someone fumbling at her forehead, trying to pluck her out of sleep.

"Insanity?"

"Oh, I doubt it. Not in view . . ."

Insanity. "I'm not," said Victoria loudly and angrily. "I'm not . . . oh, go away."

Simon Halliday stopped stroking her hair and moved blurredly into distance. Victoria's eyes followed him uncomprehendingly. The yellow corduroy wing chair, the tall gilt mirror, the flowered linen framing the black windowpanes . . . she was on the couch in the living room of the Thall house, and they must, Simon and Sergeant Tansill, have sat up all night with her. Simon, to whom she had called mutely for help. . . . She said exploringly, "When will it be light?"

Sergeant Tansill looked at his watch and made calculations. "In a little over seven hours," he said gravely.

Seven hours. It wasn't midnight then, couldn't be even an hour since ... Memory came back, like a brutal touch on raw flesh. Victoria raised her head a little and sent a glance of panic around the room, and saw Sergeant Tansill's round calm affable face looking down at her. "You're all right now, Miss Devlin. You took a running dive under the table in the darkroom, that's all, and nearly knocked your brains out. Feeling better yet?"

"Yes. But what—"

"Nothing," said Sergeant Tansill flatly. "You're going back to the East Wind and to sleep—Dr. Lemon is on his way with soothing syrup. Do you realize how nearly you were number three?"

"But I'm all right, and I want to know—"

"Tomorrow. Here's the doctor now. . . ."

And in the end she did go back to the East Wind, led by Simon and tucked in by one of the wide-eyed Misses Soames. And, incredibly, slept, although that might have been the red capsule left by Dr. Lemon. So that it was nearly three o'clock on the following afternoon before they sat, she and Simon and Sergeant Tansill, in the dim little parlor that had been turned over to them. Icicles dripped silver at the window; between potted plants Victoria could catch a glimpse of satiny sunlit water.

"I'll tell you what you have to know, and you can read the rest in the papers later," said Sergeant Tansill. "Does either of you remember the Herbert Blair affair? I don't suppose you would—that was quite a while ago, in 1941."

That was the focal point, the year for which Lilac's diary had been stolen. "The Blair case in Boston," said Tansill, "is like who-killed-Elwell with the New York police. We never found out up here who killed Blair, either. In fact, all anybody knew about Blair was that he was thirty at the time he died, quite a ladies' man, and currently operating as a traveling salesman for a stocking firm. He came originally from Chicago, but he'd been a small-time Don Juan all over the middle west, ending up, so far as the police could find out, in Pittsburgh. That was before he came to Boston on a business trip—his last."

Outside, sunlight glittered on ice. One of the Soames sisters opened the parlor a crack, said yearningly, "Would you care for some tea?" and retreated before Sergeant Tansill's brown stare. And Victoria began to listen to the ac-

count of another death, eight years ago, that had had its final and frightful echoes in Seacastle, thirty miles away.

Herbert Blair, the sergeant explained, had managed to
get a list of names and the telephone numbers of what
were sometimes referred to as "call girls;" later, after the
fatal party that came to an end in his hotel room, the police were baffledly unable to establish that any one of the
listed girls had been present. "We know now, of course,
that Blair didn't use the list. A—friend provided two young
girls who thought they were being very daring and worldly.
They were Lilac Thall, who was seventeen at the time, and
a school companion of hers, Hope Carmichael."

The tale of that long-ago evening had a simple and
sordid ending. By the early hours of the morning an un-
identified man had dropped out of the party and Blair, his
friend, Hope Carmichael and Lilac Thall had returned to
his hotel room. Blair had been drinking heavily. He made
advances to Lilac, turning uglier as her terror grew. Half
out of her mind with desperation, and acting on the
shouted advice of Blair's friend, Lilac had pulled open a
bureau drawer, snatched up the gun she found there and
fired it. Blair dropped to the floor, dead. At that point—
"I'm guessing here," said Sergeant Tansill—Hope Carmichael emerged from the adjoining bath, where she had
been ill, and was quickly told what had happened. Upon
which the three fled—Lilac Thall, in a state bordering on
hysteria, the appalled Hope, and Blair's friend, the sanest
of the trio, Olive Stacey.

Olive. The stalker in the darkroom, the malignance
behind the hideously gentle whispering. Olive.

"The case was never solved. Blair hadn't been a very
savory character, and some people assumed that he had
been shot by a wronged husband. The police inclined to a
prowler theory—the bureau drawer was still open, remember, and Blair's wallet had been removed. Anyway, Miss
Stacey had the presence of mind, afterwards, to dream up
a mythical chambermaid at the hotel who had caught a
glimpse of Lilac's face as they ran to the fire escape. For
nearly eight years," said Sergeant Tansill grimly, "Miss
Thall paid blackmail to someone who never existed at all,
through the kind and helpful agency of Olive Stacey."

And then the inevitable had happened. Lilac, desperate under the yoke, her marriage to Simon approaching
rapidly and her future happiness threatened, had demanded

that she accompany Olive to South Station, the supposed place of payment, in order that she might see the chambermaid for herself and perhaps reason with her. She had to be stopped—and she was, by means of drugs.

Simon was shaking his head. "I still don't see—"

"Don't you, Mr. Halliday? I suppose in one way that was the root of the trouble—nobody ever did see Olive Stacey, she was just there. She was just there all those years after her stepfather in Pittsburgh died and she came to stay with your aunt for a time; she was just there making herself so useful that she became an unofficial part of the family. You were starting college then, I believe, Mr. Halliday, and she was thoroughly dazzled by you—or maybe by the prospect of the Halliday funds you'd some day have. Because, you see, although she was dressed and housed and fed by your aunt, Olive Stacey never had a cent of her own. Except, of course, what she was able to extract from Lilac Thall."

Olive's cell-like room at the Halliday house—yes, thought Victoria. Why hadn't she realized before that, in the midst of luxury, it was the barren quarters of an upper servant? She sat straighter on the sedate love seat. "Lilac did get suspicious, though, after she'd been drugged. She did go to New York to see Hope and find out if there was any loop-hole. . . ."

"Yes. On last Friday night, she informs us," said Sergeant Tansill bitterly. "Do you know, Miss Devlin, that you could be charged with obstructing justice and a few other things? However, we'll let that go for the moment. Miss Thall went to New York and had quite a time locating the John Maxwell Gardners, who were playing coy with the newspapers and had gone to ground in an obscure hotel. It was Sunday night before Miss Thall found them, and Monday before she could get the former Hope Carmichael alone and find out what she'd have known all along if she'd followed the newspapers, if she hadn't gone tearing off to Bermuda."

The parlor was very still and shadowed. Simon had his head cocked, frowning. Victoria, who had started to reach for a cigarette, drew her hand back and stared and waited.

"Lilac Thall couldn't possibly have shot Herbert Blair," said Sergeant Tansill, "because he was shot through the back. The bullet from her gun must have gone harmlessly through an open window. But Miss Stacey, who had arranged the little gathering with just this in mind, fired almost simultaneously from behind a curtain, so that when Blair pitched forward at Miss Thall's feet . . ." He shrugged.

"But why?" Victoria paused, her mind going confusedly back to the snapshot she had found in the printing frame. "Did Olive kill Blair because she'd lived with him once in Pittsburgh, and he threatened to tell the Hallidays?"

"Very nearly, Miss Devlin. That idyllic interlude in a boarding-house," said Sergeant Tansill with distaste, "was followed by a civil ceremony in which Miss Stacey became Mrs. Herbert Blair. The time they spent together as husband and wife was, I gather, very brief. But you can imagine Miss Stacey's consternation when, after she was comfortably settled in a leisurely household with her sights set on Simon Halliday, her husband turned up to say that his relatives by marriage had better cut him in, too. Exit Mr. Blair. To get back to Miss Thall and her errand in New York. . . ."

Acting on information from Hope Carmichael Gardner, who said that she would deny the whole business if her name was ever brought into it, Lilac had gone to Pittsburgh, to the address where Herbert Blair was known to have lived before his trip to Boston. During all this time, Lilac had failed to make contact with the police and was terrified of having her whereabouts discovered because, if Hope were wrong, she would be convicted of murder.

Going back two addresses, Lilac finally arrived, as the police had, at a Mrs. Stoner, the proprietress of the ugly frame boarding-house in the snapshot. The police eight years ago hadn't been able to offer a heart-rending story and a diamond ring—Lilac could and did. Mrs. Stoner brought out a snapshot of a fire in her boarding-house, taken by her brother eight years ago. And the man and the woman in night clothes were, of course, Olive Stacey and Herbert Blair.

Lilac had what she wanted, then—a solid and damning link between Olive and the dead man. She also had the gun that she had shot that night, which instinct had made her keep. But she had read of Nurse Corey's death, and she was terrified of the woman whom she now knew to be a murderess twice over. She had no way of knowing that her phone call to Victoria from New York, which she had paid a taxi driver to make for her, had been listened to by Olive on the kitchen extension in the Halliday house.

"Nurse Corey knew," Victoria said slowly, feeling her way. "And Olive got nearly as far as the third-floor bedroom once, over the week-end. . . ."

"Yes. Miss Stacey undoubtedly suspected the sudden 'illness' that kept Lilac Thall in seclusion. She'd had to act precipitately when she drugged Miss Thall, and she reasoned that her victim was probably getting suspicious. I don't think," said Sergeant Tansill, "that Nurse Corey knew the whole thing."

No, thought Victoria; that was why the nurse had tried to find Lilac's diaries. But she had known enough—or said something damning enough when she came face to face with Olive on the third-floor landing, to make her own death necessary. And Olive, who like everyone else in Seacastle knew the details of William Fowler's mad, motiveless killings, had stolen the sickle from the shed in back of the house, and had somehow coaxed Nurse Corey out of the house and into the dark.

She said, feeling sick, "I suppose Olive telephoned Nurse Corey and disguised her voice. . . ."

". . . and said she had a message from Lilac. Or possibly even that she was Hope Carmichael—whatever it was, it brought Nurse Corey running. But Miss Stacey didn't know, because it hadn't been included in the newspaper accounts, that William Fowler, whose technique she was imitating, had struck and stunned his other victims first. That was what made us begin to wonder. . . It's getting on," said Sergeant Tansill abruptly. "You've heard all that matters."

"No." Victoria was firm. Somewhere in the back of her mind was the conviction that it had to be told now, and the malevolence exercised completely and for good. "It's been over a week—or eight years, in a way—since all this started to happen. You can't unscramble it all in twenty minutes."

There was another tap at the parlor door. "Are you sure you wouldn't like some tea?" asked Hester Soames, raking them all in one eager glance. "It wouldn't take but a minute. . . ."

"No tea, thank you," said Sergeant Tansill with suspicious affability. "Do you think you could spread the word?"

When the door had closed again he turned back to his listeners. "There isn't much more to tell. A lot of the details we won't find out unless Miss Stacey chooses to tell us, such as what plausible tale she told Charles Storrow to lull his suspicions while they sat and drank sherry at his house—hers straight, his with enough sedative in the initial dose to have given a jolt to a much stronger heart than his. I imagine it was she who suggested his note to Miss Thall, probably a final plea: 'I can't stand the thought of your marrying another man. . . .' Something like that."

"And it was because of the brown calf handbag that he had to be killed?"

"Yes. Because it was only a matter of time before he'd get in touch with the maid to question her about it, and chances are Miss Stacey was afraid she'd been seen disposing of it."

The sergeant listened in disapproving silence to Victoria's description of how Olive had come running into Charles Storrow's house on Blackfan Road, and had broken off in the midst of a revelation when she discovered with apparent shock, the body in the bedroom.

"Oh, she was clever," he said slowly. "Did you turn on a light when you went in, by any chance, Miss Devlin? My guess is that she got nervous about some trace she might have left there, went back, saw someone enter the house just ahead of her and decided to risk it anyway, calling his name as a blind. She took another risk, earlier, when she got in touch with Mr. Halliday's former secretary, Incidentally, Miss Reinhardt assumed that the female voice on the telephone belonged to a Miss Halliday, which caused some confusion about whom she had come to see. Anyway, she and Miss Stacey arranged a neat little plan by which Mr. Halliday could be held accountable for the leakage at the agency—the secretary, of course, being ripe for anything in the way of revenge. As I see it, this was to be a desperate last stand with Miss Thall— 'If you keep your mouth shut and agree to forget the whole business, I won't ruin your fiancé.' "

"But—how do you know all this?" Victoria was bewildered. "Miss Reinhardt, the trouble at Simon's agency . . ."

Sergeant Tansill smiled a little and looked across at Simon. "We have your brother to thank for that," he said.

"Rufus Halliday was, I think, the only other person—aside from Charles Storrow, at the end—who suspected his cousin Olive. Not so strongly that he could bring himself to make any accusation—she had, after all, been a member of the household for over ten years—but enough to make him remove the keys from both cars when he found out that she intended to visit Miss Thall last night at the hospital. That, by the way, was what made Miss Stacey late in arriving—she had to take a taxi instead of driving as she'd planned. She never entered the hospital, because she saw Miss Devlin going in, but she was able to follow Miss Devlin's taxi to the garage." The sergeant swung his brown gaze to Victoria. "When I found out you hadn't come back here, I took a chance on its being the Thall house or thereabouts. Miss Stacey made quite a racket when you dived for the floor. . . ."

Victoria felt remembered horror for an instant, pushed her mind determinedly back. Rufe's warning to drop the question of Lilac's appointment, Rufe's too-airy dismissal of Charles Storrow's queries, Rufe's charges of missing money against the maid, Esther Schultz—he had been trying to protect them all from the menace he suspected but couldn't prove. Later, instead of embracing Olive in that startling little scene Victoria had witnessed, he must have seized her wrists in an impotent and raging attempt to get the truth from her. At any rate, Sergeant Tansill was explaining, Rufe had gone to him, in his worry on Simon's behalf, to find out what credence might be given a trumped-up accusation of her employer by a woman who was known to have been fired from her job, if it should come to the question of an affidavit. . . .

And there was, suddenly, the muddy subject of the Spencers: of Freddy, whose ambitions were bigger than his salary; of Millicent, whose vicious jealousy of her younger sister had prompted her to drive in Lilac's car and kerchief through the town and to Charles Storrow's house in the hope of exposing the false situation that she was fairly certain existed.

It had been spite, blind and blundering, and later Millicent had panicked. Nevertheless it must have confused Olive badly, in the beginning. Victoria shivered a little, remembering how nearly she had been trapped into admissions by Olive's quiet, deadly cleverness. On that dreadful, fog-blurred Monday afternoon Olive had said with gentle perplexity, "Lilac phoned last night." And there had been a fleeting moment, before Victoria thought she saw speculation in the other woman's face, when the betraying words had tumbled almost to her lips.

They had all been dealing in lies and subterfuge, offering fragments of the truth now and then to make the confusion deeper. Victoria stared at an icicle dripping crystal at the window and said suddenly, "But the night Lilac was attacked, I thought Olive had been at dinner with some people. How did she—?"

"That was nice, wasn't it?" said Sergeant Tansill appreciatively. "That was really well done, I thought—until I called on the Kellermans to make sure. And one look at them would put ideas into a choir-boy's head. Mrs. Kellerman is a pretty little thing in her early thirties—and Mr. K. is pushing seventy. When I finally got the wife aside and told her we'd manage to juggle the thing a bit for Kellerman's ears, she admitted she'd been for cocktails and lingered on with an aspiring young man in her husband's law office. And yes, come to think of it, Miss Stacey *had* phoned from the house to say there was no hurry; she'd make herself comfortable with a drink and some records and have the maid put dinner off a while. After all, Mr. Kellerman was in Baltimore and what he didn't know wouldn't hurt him. . . ."

But it nearly killed Lilac, thought Victoria; Lilac, who would be well enough soon to come home and have the final fitting for her wedding dress.

"It's nearly five. I'm going home," observed Sergeant Tansill passionately to his feet, "and have Mrs. Tansill put a bit of butter and some cloves and a drop of hot water in a bottle of rum. Good-bye, Miss Devlin. I'll be seeing more of you, I think."

Victoria stared at the closing door. It had come to this—a dryness in her throat, a feeling of emptiness, a gray vacancy where future plans should be. A crisp and pleasant good-bye in a stiff little parlor—she moved toward the door, and said, "I suppose he means that I'll have to testify."

"I don't think that's what he means at all," said Simon.

"Oh. Well, I'll have to find out," Victoria said rapidly, "because I've a job to get and an aunt to reassure, among other things. And I want to talk to Lilac—have you seen her today, by the way?"

She took another careless step and Simon was there at the door, his eyes relentlessly steady on her face. He said slowly, "Yes, I've seen her. And I found out something that Lilac said she'd known for a long time. I—we liked each other a very great deal, probably more than a lot of people do after the first anniversary. But then you—" Simon stopped. His level, measuring look was gone. He had asked her something with his eyes, gravely and with an odd gentleness, before he said, "Victoria, if you knew that it had been Charles Storrow all along with Lilac, that with Storrow dead there can't be anyone else for her for a long time—would it make a difference?"

Charles Storrow, to whom Lilac had turned blindly and instinctively at the end with the mission that had almost cost Victoria her life. . . . Lilac, brought up in the luxury she loved and then stripped of it, had thought she could forget Charles and make a wealthy, companionable marriage with Simon. But Charles was dead, and Simon had asked if it would make a difference. Was there a difference between night and day, pain and the warm dissolving rush of delight? Later there would be reaction against the warped and violent thing that had brought them together, and pity for Lilac, who had lost everything and would have to start all over again. Right now there was only the wonder of saying his name, not the despairing way it had echoed inside her in the moment when she had thought she was going to die, but incredulously because she was going to live, and Simon's arms were around her as though she had always belonged there.

She said, "Simon," with a kind of astonishment.

And Simon said over her hair, "Did you know, Victoria? Did you, my darling?" and lifted her face to his.

"Tea? Oh, I *beg* your pardon," said the youngest Miss Soames, and withdrew.

HAROLD ROBBINS

25,000 People a Day Buy His Novels.

Are *You* One of Them?

_____ 81150 THE CARPETBAGGERS $2.50

_____ 81151 THE BETSY $2.50

_____ 81152 THE PIRATE $2.50

_____ 81142 THE DREAM MERCHANTS $2.50

_____ 81153 THE ADVENTURERS $2.50

_____ 81154 WHERE LOVE HAS GONE $2.50

_____ 81155 A STONE FOR DANNY FISHER $2.50

_____ 81156 NEVER LOVE A STRANGER $2.50

_____ 81157 79 PARK AVENUE $2.50

_____ 81158 THE INHERITORS $2.50

Available at bookstores everywhere, or order direct from the publisher.

Curtain

HERCULE POIROT'S LAST AND GREATEST CASE

Agatha Christie

_____80720 CURTAIN $1.95

Available at bookstores everywhere, or order direct from the publisher.

POCKET BOOKS
Department cu
1 West 39th Street
New York, N.Y. 10018

Please send me the books I have checked above. I am enclosing $_____ (please add 35¢ to cover postage and handling). Send check or money order—no cash or C.O.D.'s please.

NAME_____

ADDRESS_____

CITY _____STATE/ZIP_____

CU

POCKET BOOKS